SURF'S UP!

D0365981

"Saved by the Bell" titles include:

Mark-Paul Gosselaar: Ultimate Gold
Mario Lopez: High-Voltage Star
Behind the Scenes at "Saved by the Bell"
Beauty and Fitness with "Saved by the Bell"
Dustin Diamond: Teen Star
The "Saved by the Bell" Date Book

Hot fiction titles:

SURF'S UP!

by Beth Cruise

ALADDIN PAPERBACKS

If you purchased this book without a cover you should be aware that this book is stolen property. It was reported as "unsold and destroyed" to the publisher and neither the author nor the publisher has received any payment for this "stripped book."

Photograph and logo copyright © 1995 by National Broadcasting Company, Inc. All rights reserved. *Saved by the Bell*™ is a trademark of the National Broadcasting Company, Inc. Used under license.
Text copyright © 1995 by Aladdin Paperbacks
All rights reserved, including the right of
reproduction in whole or in part in any form
Aladdin Paperbacks
An imprint of Simon & Schuster
Children's Publishing Division
1230 Avenue of the Americas
New York, NY 10020
First Aladdin Paperbacks edition August 1995
Manufactured in the United States of America
10 9 8 7 6 5 4 3 2 1
Library of Congress Cataloging-in-Publication Data
Cruise, Beth.
Surf's up! / by Beth Cruise. — 1st Aladdin Paperbacks ed.
p. cm. — (Saved by the bell ; #20)
Summary: In their campaign against privatization of the
Palisades beaches, Jessie and the Green Teens organize a
Save the Cove Festival complete with a volleyball competition.
ISBN 0-689-80209-9
[1. Environmental protection—Fiction. 2. Beaches—Fiction.
3. Festivals—Fiction. 4. Volleyball—Fiction.] I. Title. II. Series.
PZ7.C88827Su 1995
[Fic]—dc20 95-14516

To
everyone
who's ever been
in love

Chapter 1

▲ ▼ ▲ ▼ ▲

Jessie Spano was psyched. The day was gorgeous—the California sky a perfect blue, the sun a golden glow, and the breeze gentle and sea scented. It was not only Saturday, but the Saturday she had looked forward to for a whole week. She and her mother, one of Palisades' most dedicated public defenders, were meeting Kenyon Sinclair, the superfamous Palisades lawyer, for lunch at the exclusive Half Moon Country Club.

Now, as her mother drove their car up the long winding driveway to the clubhouse, Jessie hoped that she looked as cool and relaxed as her mother did. She sure didn't feel it. Her hands were sweaty and there were butterflies playing tag in her stomach. Although she and her mom were there for lunch, there was no way she was going to be able to eat a single bite. She was too nervous. Too excited.

What thrilled her the most was that Mr. Sinclair had asked specifically to meet her. *Her!* A nobody. Oh, sure she was senior class president, an active member in both the Palisades Historical Society and Green Teens, her environmental group, and determined to have the highest grade point average at Bayside High School, but she was nothing when compared to Kenyon Sinclair.

Not only was Mr. Sinclair extremely successful, he was heavily involved with local interests such as ecology, historical preservation, and urban renewal. He regularly defended the underprivileged, spoke out in favor of women's rights and equality, and was even an alumnus of dear old Bayside. She had followed his career closely, studying it as one worthy of emulating. She had nearly fainted when her mother had told her Mr. Sinclair wanted to meet her.

The car glided to a stop before the grandly canopied entrance of the clubhouse. Before Jessie could reach for the door handle, a handsome young parking attendant opened the door and helped her out. Another good-looking guy assisted her mother. A third stood holding the clubhouse door open for them.

Everywhere she looked there were athletically

built guys in polo shirts with the Half Moon insignia on the pocket. And they were all flashing killer smiles. Kelly had worked in the Half Moon's restaurant for a brief time, but she'd never said anything about being surrounded by drop-dead gorgeous guys.

The gardens were as pleasing to the eye as the guys. Carefully cut green lawns flowed into artistically sculpted flower beds filled with masses of pink, red, yellow, white, blue, and purple blooms. More flowers, gathered in giant bouquets on highly polished tables, filled the clubhouse itself. The atmosphere was quiet and refined.

And expensive, Jessie thought after catching a glance of some members waiting to be seated in the dining room. Their clothes were so perfect, so obviously designer made, that she felt uncomfortable in her short-skirted suit.

"Relax, sweetheart," her mother said, and smiled softly. "You're here to enjoy yourself."

Jessie took a deep breath. "I'll try."

"Kate!" a man's voice called. "I'm so glad you could make it."

"Kenyon," Jessie's mother greeted him, holding out her hands to a tall man in tennis whites. "We wouldn't have missed lunching with you for the world."

Jessie watched as Kenyon Sinclair kissed her mother's cheek. He was quite a handsome man, his graying hair giving him a distinguished air, but the warm smile in his blue eyes told of a kind and caring heart. When her mother introduced them, Jessie was relieved that she managed to greet Mr. Sinclair without stuttering.

Once seated at a linen-covered table that looked out over the rolling green acres of the golf course, Kenyon kept the conversation flowing. He asked about Jessie's goals and made a few suggestions about schools and projects she might be interested in. But soon he and her mother were talking about people Jessie didn't know, and Jessie's attention drifted to the conversations around her.

"It's perfect, Desmond," an elegant woman at the next table insisted. "The beach is crescent-shaped, rather like a quarter moon. It is secluded, the sands a pearly white, and the water a cool blue."

"So you think we should push for the sale, Deidra?" Desmond asked.

"Absolutely. And we need to keep this quiet, darling," Deidra insisted. "If word got out that the city was contemplating selling the cove, we would not be the only developers interested. The price would go sky-high in a bidding war. And we don't want that."

"True," Desmond murmured. "What did you say the locals call this place? I'd like to check it out for myself."

"Excellent idea. Of course we'll have to change

the name. Something as trite and common as Smuggler's Cove would never appeal to the exclusive guests visiting our health spa and resort," Deidra said as she got to her feet. "Shall I go with you, Desmond?"

Jessie missed Desmond's response. She was so stunned at the news that Smuggler's Cove was about to be sold that she forgot she was only pretending to be eating and stabbed a fork full of lettuce.

"How's your salad, Jessie?" Kenyon Sinclair asked.

"Uh, fine. Great," Jessie hurried to assure him.

"Are you sure, sweetheart?" her mother said. "You've hardly eaten a thing."

"No, really. It's fine," Jessie insisted, and hastily ate the lettuce on her fork. She was relieved when the adults turned their attention away from her.

She had to have heard wrong, Jessie told herself. There was no way the city government could sell Smuggler's Cove. It was a public beach and the most beautiful place in the world. Everyone who saw it loved the cove. Deidra was quite right in saying the sand was pearly white. It looked especially so in the moonlight, which also made it Palisades's most romantic spot.

But if what she had overheard was true, Smuggler's Cove would soon be romantic for only a very few people, those able to pay to stay at Desmond and Deidra's exclusive resort and health spa.

Forgetting she was too excited to eat, Jessie chewed on another mouthful of salad and thought about every time she had enjoyed the peace and beauty of Smuggler's Cove. As beautiful as it was, the beach was not visited frequently, mostly because, from the road, it was a steep climb down a cliff path to reach it. The gently curved beach was sheltered from the wind by two outcroppings of hills. She had taken illegal alien Ramón Calderón there to hide him from immigration agents. But her fondest memories were of walks along the sands with Slater, her hand in his, the promise of a tender shared kiss on their minds. Once it had been their special place, where they went when they needed to talk or just be alone and watch the moonlight dance on the waves.

Since she and Slater had decided to be just friends—a big mistake as far as she was concerned—Smuggler's Cove had come to represent the time they had spent together as boyfriend and girlfriend. If she could no longer go to Smuggler's Cove to dream, she'd go crazy.

Well, that wasn't going to happen. Nobody took away Jessie Spano's dreams. She would fight the sale of Smuggler's Cove. She'd get the gang to help her. She'd enlist the support of Green Teens. Of Bayside. Of the residents of Palisades itself!

Across the table from her, Kenyon Sinclair

glanced at his watch. "I'm sorry Kate, Jessie," he said. "As much as I've enjoyed lunching with you both, I've got a meeting with some contractors in the historical district. Jessie, if you have any problems I can help you with, just let me know. Kate, I'll see you in court." When her mother laughed, he flashed her a mischievous smile and a tender look.

Jessie nearly choked on a piece of broccoli. Oh my gosh! It looked like Kenyon was interested in more than just offering her advice on a career in the law. He was interested in a romance with her mother!

Apparently he didn't know about Chance Gifford, her mom's boyfriend in New Mexico. Chance owned the Lazybones Ranch, a dude ranch outside of Santa Fe.

But now that she thought about it, Chance hadn't flown in for a visit in a long time, and his calls weren't as frequent as they'd once been. Did that mean that their long-distance romance had fizzled? It seemed impossible. Chance and her mother had always looked so much in love.

"Ready to leave, Jess?" Kate Spano asked. "If you'd like, we could do some mother-daughter shopping at the mall. That's something we don't often get an opportunity to do."

That was true. Jessie usually went to the mall with Lisa and Kelly.

It sure didn't sound like her mother was suffering from a broken heart. Unless she had fallen out of love with Chance already. Maybe she didn't really want to shop but wanted to simply explain that she wasn't seeing Chance anymore. Maybe she even wanted to find out what Jessie thought of Kenyon Sinclair!

"Sure! Sounds great!" Jessie agreed, her mind running in frantic circles. There were so many things she needed to think about! Smuggler's Cove, Chance and her mom, Kenyon and her mom.

Golly! And she'd thought she was excited before lunch!

▲　▼　▲

Lisa Turtle slid into the seat across from Jessie at the Max, the gang's regular hangout. "Look at you, girl!" Lisa insisted. "You're a mess!"

Jessie looked up. Her elbows were on the table, her hands were buried in her long brown curls, and she was grinding her teeth. There was also a giant double chocolate malt in front of her. When stressed out, Jessie went for chocolate in a big way.

"Ah, at last! Help," Jessie murmured, and sat up straighter.

"Easy for you to say," Lisa said. "It may take a case of conditioner to get those knots out of your hair."

"I'm not talking about my hair," Jessie said. "I've got problems. Did you manage to get hold of Kelly?"

Lisa smiled in satisfaction. "Not only Kelly but Zack, Slater, and Screech. They'll all be here."

A. C. Slater was the first one to walk through the Max's front door. With his curly black hair and dimples, he looked as good as the handsome Half Moon parking attendants. But the sight of him brought the fate of Smuggler's Cove all too clearly to mind. Jessie grabbed her malt and slurped.

"What's up?" he asked, sliding into the booth next to Jessie. "Lisa made it sound like a four-alarm fire."

"It is. Sort of," Jessie said.

Kelly Kapowski swung through the door, the short skirt of her tennis dress flipping flirtatiously as she hopped down the steps toward them. A guy at the next table got distracted as he watched her, forgot to pay attention to where he was pouring catsup, missed his burger, and covered his lap with red goop.

"Hi!" Kelly greeted brightly.

"You sure look happy," Slater said.

"I am," Kelly agreed, and took a seat next to Lisa. "I just beat Zack three out of four sets in tennis. Think I should join the Bayside team?"

"Only if you're planning on playing guys," Jessie said. "I'll bet Zack didn't have his eyes on the ball very often."

Kelly giggled. "Well," she admitted, tossing her long dark hair back over her shoulder, "he did seem to think my new outfit showed off my tan nicely."

Zack Morris and Samuel "Screech" Powers arrived together, tried to come through the door at the same time, and got stuck. It was only after Zack shoved his wildly dressed, geeky friend into the room ahead of him that they joined the rest of the gang in their regular booth.

"The marines have landed," Zack announced, stealing a chair from the adjacent table and spinning it around to straddle it.

"They have?" Screech croaked, leaning on the back of the booth near Lisa. "I didn't hear anything about it on the news."

"I mean us, Screech," Zack explained. "What's the rush, Jess? I was busy helping Kelly with her tennis game."

"So we heard, preppie," Slater said. "You look a little tired. Chase a few too many balls to the back of the court?"

Zack cocked one blond eyebrow. "I let her win," he said, leaning toward Slater and lowering his voice so the others wouldn't overhear. "A morale-building exercise."

"Oh, sure," Slater whispered back.

Jessie pushed her empty malt glass away. "I've got some megabad news, guys," she said. "It looks like the city is planning on selling Smuggler's Cove to some private developers."

"They can't!" Kelly insisted.

"No!" Lisa wailed. "Not when I finally talked Keith into having a picnic there. It's the most romantic place I know."

Lisa had only recently begun dating Keith Bockman, who was not only a shy yet gorgeous hunk, but the Bayside tennis champ.

"Who told you Smuggler's Cove is up for sale?" Slater asked.

Jessie bit her bottom lip. "Well, no one actually *told* me. I overheard a couple talking about it at the Half Moon—"

Zack frowned. "What were you doing at that place? Didn't we all agree to boycott it after the way they treated Kelly?"

"No," Lisa corrected. "*You* decided to boycott it. It would have been ridiculous for me to do so considering my parents spent a small fortune to join."

"That's true," Screech announced, backing her up.

"Besides," Lisa said, "the Half Moon is under new management, and a number of changes have been made since you got Brad Porterhouse fired for harassing Kelly."

"So that's why all those great-looking guys are working there now," Jessie mused.

Slater's eyes narrowed slightly. "What great-looking guys?"

"The—"

Zack cut her off. "What were you doing there, Jess?" he demanded.

"Other than enjoying the hunky scenery," Lisa added.

Jessie leaned forward. "Well, Mom and I were invited to lunch by Kenyon Sinclair—"

"Not that gorgeous lawyer I saw on the news last night!" Kelly squealed. "Oh, Jess. Is he as handsome in person? And his voice. Is it really that sexy?"

Jessie sighed. "Is it ever. I think he's got a thing for Mom and—"

Zack cleared his throat. "Smuggler's Cove, Jess."

"Oh, right. Well, Kenyon and Mom were talking about cases and my mind started to wander and that's when I overheard them."

"Them," Zack repeated.

"Desmond and Deidra."

"Desmond and Deidra who?" Slater asked.

"I don't know. That's just what I heard them call each other. But they were talking about rushing through a sale of Smuggler's Cove so they could open a very exclusive resort and health spa there," Jessie said.

"A health spa?" Lisa echoed, perking up. "What kind of health spa? A fancy European beauty one? It would be really great to have one near, wouldn't it?"

"Yeah," Kelly admitted sadly. "If you can afford to visit it. I'd never get to see Smuggler's Cove ever again, though."

"Me neither," Screech said. "I wouldn't have a reason to go. Natural beauty runs in my family." He struck a pose, allowing them all to admire his profile.

"Yeah, right," Lisa mumbled. "So when is this

sale supposed to go through?"

"I don't know," Jessie admitted.

"Whose idea was it to sell the beach?" Slater asked.

Jessie shrugged. "I don't know."

"Why is the city even considering selling it?" Zack asked.

Jessie sighed deeply. "I just don't know."

The gang exchanged looks.

"So, what do you want us to do?" Slater asked.

"Stop them?" Jessie suggested in a small voice. "Please?"

Chapter 2

▲ ▼ ▲ ▼ ▲

"You know," Zack mused, "this might not be as easy as some of the things we've done in the past."

"Like what?" Jessie asked.

"Like when we replaced the designer dress Mr. Belding bought for his wife after it got ruined when Lisa tried it on," he said. Mr. Belding was the principal at Bayside and a frequent victim of Zack's scams.

"It didn't get ruined simply because I tried it on," Lisa growled, "it was because—"

Zack wasn't listening, though. "Or the time when Kelly was the Piglet Pop Princess and we had to rescue her from the kidnappers."

"They had already decided to let me go, so I wasn't in need of rescuing," Kelly pointed out.

"Well, how about the time we had to sneak Marian Lenihan's missing ruby earring back into her house before she had us arrested for stealing it?" Zack said.

"That was easy?" Screech asked in amazement.

"So what you're saying, preppie, is this might be more than we can handle?" Slater demanded. "Sounds pretty straightforward to me."

Jessie looked at him in astonishment. "It does?"

"Sure. First off, you don't know for sure if the city is planning to sell the cove," he said.

"But I heard—"

"Hearsay. You of all people know you need facts before drawing conclusions, momma. Look what happened when you suspected foul play at the Lazybones Ranch," Slater reminded her.

Jessie swallowed loudly. Not only had she nearly ruined her mother's romance with Chance, she'd lost Slater as a boyfriend and still hadn't managed to win him back.

"Okay," she agreed. "We need to find out for sure that the beach is being sold."

"And why," Lisa added. "There might be a very good reason, you know."

"Or a nefarious one," Screech said, screwing his rubbery face into a sly grimace and rubbing his chin thoughtfully. "A bit of skulking at city hall and—"

Kelly shook her head. "Who needs to skulk? You're a computer whiz, Screech. As an expert

surfer on the information highway, you can probably find out what we need to know without going
near downtown."

"Hey, isn't that illegal?" Slater asked.

"Heck, no," Zack insisted. "To make sure the
sale of the cove is totally legal the city would have
to put the proposal on paper. Probably buried in
with a lot of other business so it wouldn't be spotted
easily. And all of that stuff is public information. All
Screech has to do is word search any reference to
Smuggler's Cove."

Screech nodded. "It's a cinch," he said, and
tried to snap his fingers. They ended up looking
more like he'd tried to tie them in a knot.

"And if Screech finds out that what Jessie heard
is true?" Lisa asked. "Then what?"

"Then phase two," Slater said.

Kelly propped her chin in her hands. "What's
phase two?"

Slater grinned across the table at her. "What
else?" he asked. "We unleash our secret weapon."

Jessie frowned. "What secret weapon?"

"Zack," Slater said. "Who else?"

▲ ▼ ▲

Zack sat on the cliff edge, Kelly at his side.
Below them was the pretty crescent-shaped beach
of Smuggler's Cove.

Bringing Kelly to the superromantic setting
before taking her home had been a stroke of pure

genius. She was feeling sentimental about the place, already picturing it in the hands of mercenary developers. He'd slowly been regaining lost ground the last few months. After writing love poetry for her, he had been sure she'd agree to go steady with him once again. But Kelly had surprised him by refusing to give an answer when he asked, and Zack knew why.

His scams.

They had gotten him in hot water often enough. Especially with Kelly, considering they'd involved another girl each time. Having decided that she was the only girl he wanted in his life had made Zack determined to give up scamming. Or to scam only when she approved.

Or when she wouldn't catch him at it.

Perhaps if he saved Smuggler's Cove she'd finally promise to be his girl. Being a hero was fairly romantic stuff, after all. It might be just the ticket to her heart.

Down below, the tide was coming in, which pretty well ruined any chance of a stroll along the beach. But the sight of the sun glinting on the water and the sound of the rushing surf were special, too. The taste of salt was strong in the air, but it was the scent of Kelly's flowery perfume that filled Zack's head.

It was time, he decided, to play the sensitive man.

Zack took Kelly's hand and entwined his fingers with hers. "You don't mind that Jessie asked

for my help, do you?" he asked. "I know how much
you hate it when I run a scam."

Kelly squeezed his hand lightly. "That's only
because you do it behind my back more often than
not. But I don't see what else can be done," she
admitted. "I really do hate it when you scam, but
sometimes it does seem to be the only answer. And
you are awfully good at it. Most of the time."

"What if you thought of it as more of a plan
than a scam?" Zack suggested.

"You mean no trickery?"

Well, that was asking a lot of a guy. If it came to
making promises, he'd have to avoid that particular
one.

"Suppose we just get a lot of people involved?
Make sure all of Palisades know the beach is about
to be taken away from them," Zack suggested,
thinking quickly.

Kelly smiled brightly at him. "And if enough
people protest, then the sale can't go through?" she
asked eagerly.

"Something like that."

Hmm. Maybe that *would* work, he mused, then
decided to play it safe and stall for time.

"Naturally we can't do anything until we know
the reason behind the sale," he said.

"Zack," Kelly murmured thoughtfully. "Do you
think someone in the city government is being paid
by Desmond and Deidra to arrange it?"

"Could be." It would certainly be the kind of scam he pictured someone like Brandon Jarrett, the father of one of Zack's past flings, pulling. Once he'd thought the man a brilliant scammeister. But after seeing how unhappy Brandon was as an adult still trying to pull off deals through trickery, Zack had changed his mind about life as a con artist.

Of course he still didn't know what to do with his future since making that awesome decision. It would come to him, though. And as long as no one was hurt by his scams, planning them kept his agile mind . . . well, agile.

Kelly leaned her head on his shoulder. "This is such a beautiful place, I can see someone doing almost anything to own it."

"Hmm," Zack agreed, resting his cheek against her soft, shiny hair. A few more minutes and Smuggler's Cove would have woven its magic and kissing her would be a cinch.

As if she read his mind, Kelly sighed and slipped away from Zack. "Well, we can't do anything more until Screech finds out what's going on," she said, and scrambled to her feet. "You know, it's so nice here, I hate to leave, but I've got to get home. It's my night to help Mom with dinner."

Yep, he definitely had to pull this one off, Zack decided, reluctantly getting to his feet. Scamming for the good of the community had to win Kelly back to his side. Forever he hoped.

▲ ▼ ▲

Screech reported in to Jessie the next afternoon. The city was definitely planning on selling Smuggler's Cove. He'd found a memo on the proposal buried at the end of a long agenda. In it, a council member claimed that since Smuggler's Cove was too remote for easy public access, selling it would be justified to provide much-needed funds to rehabilitate the more accessible and frequented city parks.

Everything about the proposal seemed legal and logical.

But that didn't make it right.

Jessie called another emergency meeting at the Max. The whole gang was crammed in their usual booth fifteen minutes later.

"So what do you suggest we do, Zack?" she demanded, pinning him with an eagle-sharp look.

Zack resisted the urge to squirm. "I don't know why you need me to think up a solution," he insisted. She didn't need to know he hadn't had a brainstorm yet.

"That's true," Kelly said. "Why, yesterday when we went out to Smuggler's Cove, Zack mentioned that all we might need to do is protest the sale to kill the deal."

"No one knows more about protesting than you do, momma," Slater murmured. Jessie had dragged him off to enough Green Teens protests in the past to convince him that she was an expert.

"Yeah," Lisa agreed. "If you just get your environmental friends involved, Smuggler's Cove will be saved in nothing flat."

"And if you march in front of the courthouse," Screech added, "I'll be right there with you, Jessie. How many news crews do you think will be covering us when we're dragged off to jail? I've always wanted to be on television."

Jessie glared at him. "We won't be dragged off to jail, Screech."

He looked disappointed but rallied. "Well, I'll do it anyway," he offered.

"Using the Green Teens members is a good idea," Jessie said. "But it will take a few days to call an emergency meeting. We need to be doing something now to hold up the sale. Desmond and Deidra sounded like they were in an awful hurry to rush the sale through immediately. What if they manage to do it while we're stuck in school tomorrow?"

Everyone stared at her. If a vote had been taken on extending the school year, Jessie would have been the only one in favor of doing so. To hear her bemoaning school was scary!

Jessie turned frantic eyes on Zack. "You've got to pull something off to slow them down," she pleaded.

"Hey! I've got to be in school tomorrow, too," he reminded her. "It may have escaped your notice, but Mr. Belding keeps a close eye on my whereabouts. If I'm missing, he'll probably come looking for me."

"Or call your parents," Kelly added.

Zack winced. "Anything but that."

"There's got to be something that can be done," Lisa insisted. "Didn't you get any bright ideas when you went to the beach yesterday?"

"We didn't get a chance to get down to the beach," Zack said.

"The tide was coming in," Kelly explained. "It was pretty deserted."

"Which is why the city is planning to sell it," Slater murmured. "It should be low tide right now. How about if we scope it out for ourselves. It might be our last chance."

"Oh, don't say that!" Lisa moaned. "It sounds so final."

"Well, I'm going to enjoy the place while I still can," Slater said. He slid out of the booth and paused. "Coming with me, momma?" he asked Jessie, and held out his hand to her.

Jessie hesitated for a single heartbeat before slipping her hand in his. "Yeah," she said. "I'll go with you."

Chapter 3

▲ ▼ ▲ ▼ ▲

The tide was indeed out, leaving a long, freshly swept stretch of pearl white sand in its wake. Out beyond the curve of beach, waves rose in magnificent curls that hurried toward the cove, and were gentled to a soft rush of water that lapped at the shore. Seagulls soared above or sat sunning themselves on the sun-washed rocks. There wasn't a human being as far as the eye could see, until the gang arrived.

Slater and Jessie were the first ones down the cliff path, the first to shed their shoes and walk barefoot into the shallow surf. Zack and the others were only steps behind and kicking off their own shoes when Jessie let out a screech.

"Eeekkkk!"

Slater was already up to his knees in the water, but at Jessie's cry, he spun and raced back to her. "What is it?" he gasped in concern.

Jessie's eyes were wild. She pointed to the sand, her hand shaking nervously.

Slater didn't look down. He stared into her suddenly pale face. "Were you stung by a jellyfish?" he asked quickly, worried about her. The spines of a jellyfish were painful and dangerous.

Jessie shook her head no and continued to point wordlessly at the sand.

Zack and the others rushed up. "Did you cut your foot on a broken piece of seashell?" Kelly asked. Some shells were sharp enough to do major damage.

"Eww!" Lisa said with a shiver just at the thought. "I'll go get the first aid kit."

"No," Jessie insisted, at last finding her voice. "Look!"

This time they all followed the direction of her pointing finger. There in the drying sand was a footprint. Just one.

"Whoa! Talk about your déjà vu!" Zack said. "This makes me feel like I'm back in Mrs. Simpson's English class."

Lisa groaned. "Eww! I remember. We had to read that book about the guy who was stranded on a deserted island . . ."

"With the Skipper, the Professor, and . . . ," Screech began.

Lisa ignored him and kept talking. ". . . and thought he was all alone until one day he found a human footprint in the sand."

"Oh, yeah. I remember that story," Kelly said.

"And when he found the dude who'd made the print," Slater continued, picking up the story, "he—"

"He named him Friday because he'd found him on a Friday," Zack finished.

Screech squinted as he thought about it all. "But today is Sunday, so we'll have to name our mysterious footprint maker Sunday."

"Yeah, right," Lisa drawled. "Screech, we're not on a deserted island; we're ten minutes away from the heart of Palisades. This footprint was probably made by someone just like us who want- ed to enjoy the afternoon and Smuggler's Cove."

Screech tried to look sly. "Ah, but none of us is one-footed," he pointed out, "so this may well be the notorious One Foot, the mysterious, hairy beast that—"

"You mean Bigfoot," Kelly said, trying to be helpful.

Screech looked down at the imprint in the sand. "I'll say!" he agreed. The footprint was nearly twice the size of one of Lisa's dainty feet, and half again larger than any of the boys' feet.

"It was probably left by someone jogging along the beach," Slater said. "The tide just washed the other prints away."

"Or," Zack offered mischievously, "it was left by the ghost of a one-legged pirate who buried his smuggled treasure somewhere around here and was checking on it."

Kelly giggled appreciatively. "Then we have all the more reason to save Smuggler's Cove. We certainly wouldn't want the developers to find the treasure."

"Then again," Slater said, "the footprint just might have been left by one of them." He pointed out to sea, where colorful dots had appeared atop the curling waves.

Jessie sighed deeply in relief as she recognized the dots. "Surfers. Of course. Why didn't I think of that?"

"Well, you do seem a bit excitable lately," Lisa said. "Is something else bothering you besides the fate of Smuggler's Cove?"

Jessie moaned sorrowfully. "Oh, is it ever! I think that Mom might be—"

"Aloha!" a girl's voice called.

Jessie and the gang spun to face the newcomer. She was very tall, extremely blond, deeply tanned, muscularly pumped, and skimpily dressed in a bright yellow-and-orange bikini. Under her arm she carried a long surfboard painted in hot pink, glow-in-the-dark lime, and seawater blue swirls.

"Hel-lo, momma," Slater drawled appreciatively under his breath and gave her a wide smile, his dimples flashing.

Zack ran a hand over his sun-streaked blond hair, checking on its perfection, and grinned. "Aloha, gorgeous," he said, unaware that Kelly sent a swift glare his way.

"Sunday!" Screech cried in greeting, obviously missing the fact that the surfer girl's feet were a lot smaller than the footprint in the sand.

Zack rolled his eyes in exasperation and grabbed his friend before Screech could rush head-long to embrace the magnificent surfette.

Screech was unfazed. He pointed to his chest. "Me Screech," he said by way of introduction.

"Valleys," she muttered as if disgusted, and planted her surfboard in the sand, making it look rather like a colorful tombstone.

"Valleys?" Lisa repeated, confused by the term.

Zack gave the blond girl an even wider smile. "She means we're inlanders, that we don't live on the beach," he explained.

"And she does?" Lisa hissed behind his back at Kelly.

"Yeah, probably under a rock," Kelly growled back, her fingers itching to pinch Zack to remind him of her existence.

"What do you valleys want?" the surfer girl snarled. "This is like our beach, you know?"

Jessie pushed in front of the still grinning Slater. "This is a public beach," she insisted. "But it won't be for long. Were you aware that the city is planning on selling it?"

"No way," the shapely surfer said.

"Way," Zack said, angling in front of Jessie. He gazed out to sea a moment before turning back to the blond beach bunny. "Awesome rollers."

"Rollers?" Lisa looked at Kelly. "Is he kidding? I don't think that bleached mane of hers has ever spent time in hot rollers, much less ever been styled."

"He means the waves," Slater explained. "Rollers are what the dudes out there are riding."

The blond shrugged. "Killer spillers in Waikiki," she said of the waves in Hawaii. "You look more like an asphalt surfer . . ."

"Skateboarder," Slater translated.

". . . than an amped up . . ."

"Excited."

". . . boardhead."

"Surfer."

Lisa shook her head as if dizzy. "How do you know all this stuff?"

"Self-defense," Slater murmured, a twinkle in his deep brown eyes. "I had to learn to speak surfish when my family moved to Palisades even if I'm little more than a wish was."

"Wish was?" Kelly echoed.

"Would-be surfer," he explained.

"I wish I was someplace else," Lisa said.

Screech gazed happily at the shapely blond, his expression dreamy and even goofier than usual.

"Isn't Sunday perfect?" he said with a sigh.

Kelly's eyes were on Zack as he talked to the muscle-bound girl, surfer words dripping like honey from his tongue. "It started out to be a nice day," she grumbled, "but it's getting progressively worse."

"I think he means her," Lisa said.

"Oh, not Screech, too!" Kelly moaned. "What's she got that we haven't?"

"The guys' full attention," Jessie said. "She doesn't seem too interested in whether this beach is sold or not."

"I don't think she is smart enough to understand regular English," Kelly growled jealously. Zack had moved on to compliment the girl on her surfboard now.

"She probably didn't believe you," Lisa said. "Even I have trouble believing the city would deprive us of all this beauty," she added, gazing around at the tall cliff, the curve of sandy beach, the blue sky, the vastness of the ocean—and the gorgeous surfer dude who strolled through the shallows toward them, his board under his arm.

"Ahooooo!" he shouted, shaking his head and spraying everyone with water from his longish, sun-streaked, light brown hair. "Epic comber, Inga," he insisted.

Lisa sighed loudly. "I feel like I'm in a foreign country without a phrase book."

"We are, in a way," Jessie said. "Although we go

to the beach a lot, we don't hang around with surfers, so—"

The blond girl started to say something to her dripping friend, then noticed that he was no longer paying attention to her. She frowned, her forehead wrinkling into tiny frozen waves.

"Ay, caramba!" the surfer dude breathed reverently.

Figuring one of the other surfers had just done something fantastic or that a really awesome wave was building, everyone looked toward the ocean. The rest of the guys on surfboards were in calmer waters; some were already paddling back out to sea to catch the next wave. And all the waves looked pretty much as usual.

Wondering what had impressed him so, Lisa glanced back at the surfer. He was staring at her— just at her. The sun glinted off the water, clinging to his muscular chest and shoulders. The warm tan of his skin made his light blue eyes electric in color. And best of all, those wonderful eyes were glowing at her with appreciation.

"Gosh. I think I know what he just said," Lisa whispered breathlessly to Jessie and Kelly.

"I would hope so," Jessie said. "It was Spanish, and you've been taking it for three years now."

Kelly jogged Jessie's elbow. "Not literally," she insisted. "She means he likes her."

The surfer's grin was very white in his tanned face, and very wide.

"Likes her a lot," Kelly added.

Inga, the blond, wasn't happy to have her friend's attention elsewhere, though. "Bag it, Ram," she snarled. "They're valleys."

"Sweet," Ram said.

Lisa glowed. "He thinks I'm sweet," she gushed.

"Sweet means cool, Lise," Slater explained.

"Well, I think he's cool, too," she said.

Ram's grin grew wider.

"You just said he was hot. Sweet means cool, but cool means hot," Slater pointed out.

"Is he ever," Lisa agreed, grinning back at the hunky surfer.

"Chill out, Ram," Inga snapped. "Wilma there"—she indicated Jessie—"says the cove is being sold."

Jessie's jaw nearly dropped open in astonishment. "I thought you didn't believe me," she said.

Inga shrugged her muscular shoulders. Screech sighed with pleasure. "Mellow out, huh? What's not to believe? Bits of paradise get sold everywhere."

"Maybe so, but we intend to make sure this little bit of it doesn't get sold," Jessie said.

"Unreal," Ram murmured.

"No, I mean it," Jessie insisted. "We're going to stop the sale."

Slater edged up next to Jessie. "He means he thinks saving the beach is hot."

"As in good?" Jessie asked.

"I wish we all spoke the same language," Kelly said. "This conversation would be much easier without the necessity of a translator."

"Guava," Ram said.

Lisa gazed up at him. "Oh, I'm sorry. We didn't bring a picnic. And even if we had, there probably wouldn't have been any guavas in it."

"Lise?"

She turned to Slater. "Oh, don't tell me. He meant something else entirely, didn't he?"

"It was just another way of saying cool," Zack translated.

"No, dude," Ram said, "it's like I'm megafamished, and Inga has got the food stashed somewhere."

▲　▼　▲

Once Ram was happily feasting, everyone sat down in a circle and Inga got down to business. "So, which of you is the leader of this crusade for the cove? Is it you, pseud?" she asked Zack. "Or is it the wilma?"

"My name is Jessie," Jessie informed her a bit angrily. "And Zack is not a pseudosurfer, as you are implying."

Inga smiled but not nicely. "You valleys," she muttered. "I recognized all of you immediately. You're all types of inlander. He's a rev-head," she said, motioning to Slater, "more interested in cars even if he's memorized surf slang. Squid lips over there . . ." She indicated Screech, who not only didn't seem to mind the derogatory name but got an even more besotted look on his rubbery face. ". . . is a total geek. And the barbies just tag along for the ride."

"Barbies!" Kelly fumed, glaring at the surfer girl.

"Hey, I like beach barbies," Ram said.

"He likes beach barbies," Lisa repeated with a sigh of contentment.

"None of you look like you've got any pull with the big men in town," Inga continued, "so how do you propose to keep this beach out of private hands?"

"Uhhhh." Jessie looked frantically at Zack.

"By getting everybody we meet together to protest the sale," he said smoothly.

"Picketing city hall? Signing petitions?" Inga sneered at such ideas.

"No," Zack drawled, stretching out his legs and leaning back on his elbows in the sand. "I was thinking more of gathering everyone together here at Smuggler's Cove."

"Place ud be zooed out," Ram said.

Slater turned to Lisa and Kelly. "He said—"

"It would be crowded," Kelly finished for him. "I think I'm starting to get the hang of this."

"And what is the mob going to do?" Inga demanded.

"Enjoy themselves," Zack said. "The more people we get involved, the bigger this thing can be."

Inga still wasn't inclined to be overly friendly. "And just how would all these people be enjoying themselves at the cove? We don't exactly want them shoulder hopping."

When Slater didn't automatically offer to translate this time, Kelly elbowed him in the ribs. "Oh, uh, she means stealing waves."

"Thank you," Kelly said, but she was far from pleased. Zack had moved closer to Inga.

"We're still in the planning stages," Zack admitted, "and most definitely open to all suggestions. So, how do you enjoy yourself here at Smuggler's Cove?"

"Surfing," Inga said.

"And if the surf isn't pumping?" Zack asked.

"If it isn't high enough," Slater mumbled for Kelly and Lisa's benefit before he got an elbow in his ribs again.

"We still surf, dude," Ram said.

"And if there are too many guys out?"

"Ocean's crowded," Slater translated.

Ram wiped guava juice from his chin. "Only one thing to do then, dude," he insisted. "Volleyball."

Chapter 4

▲ ▼ ▲ ▼ ▲

Lisa wrinkled her nose. "Volleyball?"

"You play?" Ram asked enthusiastically. "I'm like passmodious . . ."

All the gang turned to Slater to find out what that word meant, but all he could do was shrug, admitting it surpassed his surfish knowledge.

"It means really tired," Inga said, taking pity on them.

". . . but I could play a game or two if you dudes and babes are up to it," Ram finished.

When the gang hesitated, Inga's smile curved wider. "In fact," she said, "there's nothing like a game of volleyball to settle territory rights."

Zack's grin slipped a bit. "Territory rights?"

"Oh, we're willing to do what's necessary to keep the cove out of private hands," Inga said, "but we don't want to actually share this place with inlanders."

"Why not?" Jessie demanded. "We've got just as much right to enjoy Smuggler's Cove as you do."

Inga ignored her. "What do you say to a volleyball game? Us against the six of you."

Screech frowned and rubbed his chin in thought. "It doesn't seem quite fair, Sunday," he said. "Six of us against just two of you."

"Against six of us, squid lips," Inga corrected. "Winner of two out of three games gets control of the cove."

"What!" Jessie screeched.

But before she could do anything more, Zack had extended his hand to Inga. "Shake on the deal?" he asked.

Inga did so gladly. "Ram, wave Kona, King, Fritz, and Prudence in. I'll go get the net."

"Wait!" Jessie gasped. "The rest of us didn't agree to this."

"Volleyball?" Lisa hissed at Kelly. "I don't know how to play volleyball."

Inga overheard. Her smile was so wide, the sun glancing off her teeth was enough to blind a beachcomber half a mile away. She pushed to her feet in one smooth, athletic movement. "You backing out already?"

"Not a bit," Zack assured her, scrambling to his feet. "But we're not playing you just yet."

"Then when?" Inga demanded, her brow getting all rippled again as she frowned.

"At the festival," Zack said.

Inga's scowl grew just as quickly as her smile had widened. "What festival?"

"You want I should call the dudes in?" Ram asked.

"What festival?" Jessie echoed the beach blond. "And I'm not willing to have the fate of Smuggler's Cove resting on a stupid vol—"

Slater put his hand over her mouth, effectively cutting her off. "Easy, momma. Preppie's on to something here," he murmured near her ear.

"Wamph?" Jessie said.

"Shh," Slater warned. "Just listen."

The gang all recognized Zack's manner, the Mr. Sincerity act. He was deep in scam country, exactly where they wanted him to be.

"According to our findings," Zack said, "the reason the cove is up for sale is that the city budget is short when it comes to maintenance on the parks. And where money is involved, we could all protest until we were blue in the face . . ."

"Been there," Ram told Lisa. "Wave pushed me way under. So far, I was sure I'd be seein' King Neptune himself."

". . . and the city would still sell because they

need the bucks. But if we organize a festival, invite all of Palisades to support a Save the Cove fund, and entertain them with a surfers versus valleys volleyball game, we just might raise enough money to make the city rethink their original plan," Zack explained.

Ram stared at him. "So, do you want me to call the dudes in or not?" he asked.

"Not yet, bro," Zack said. "What about it, Inga? Have we got a deal?"

"How are you going to guarantee that if we win, other inlanders will stay away?" the surfette demanded. "Seems to me that if they all troop down here to watch us play, they'll want to come back. You can't guarantee that they'll stay away."

"I couldn't guarantee it if we played right this minute, either," Zack pointed out. "But how often do you see valleys on this beach? Smuggler's Cove is one stylin' place, but it's not as easy to get to as beaches farther up the coast. They might come for a special festival, but they aren't likely to go to the trouble to come back."

"You got a point, pseud," Inga said. "It's a deal."

▲   ▼   ▲

Jessie waited until the gang had climbed back up the cliff path before she exploded. "Are you nuts, Zack? We can't play those Neanderthals at volleyball and win."

Screech still had a dreamy look on his face. "I think I'd like to move to Neanderthalia," he murmured wistfully. "You know, until meeting Sunday and Ram, I thought the term Neanderthal referred only to our prehistoric ancestors." He turned a blissful smile on Slater. "And, of course, it's Jessie's pet name for you," he said. "Now that I've met Ram and my beloved, I see that they are wonderful examples of a foreign culture of which I was totally unaware." He got a thoughtful expression on his face. "Now, why do you suppose they call their native language surfish instead of Neanderthalish?"

"Screech?" Lisa said gently. "There is no Neanderthalia. They're just surfers. Not your everyday run-of-the-mill surfers, of course. More like magnificent, I'd say. Especially Ram." She had a rather dreamy look on her own face, too.

"Earth to Lisa," Kelly called. "Excuse me for interrupting this daydream, but aren't you dating Keith Bockman?"

Lisa didn't descend from her fantasy heights. "Yes. Did you see the way Ram's muscles rippled when he moved? Say, do you think Ram is his real name? I can't really picture a mother naming her baby after a sheep."

"Who cares?" Jessie demanded. "Do you know what is going to happen when we lose all three of those volleyball games?"

"Actually," Slater said, "we don't have to lose all three games. Once we lose the first two, we won't have to play the third game."

"And after we lose, we'll never be able to enjoy a moonlight stroll at Smuggler's Cove ever again," Kelly moaned. "Oh, why did you agree to such a thing, Zack?"

"Did you hear what Sunday called me?" Screech asked. "Squid lips. Isn't that the sweetest name you've ever heard?"

"When was the last time you looked closely at a squid's lips?" Slater asked.

Zack swung himself up onto the hood of his white Mustang convertible. It was a classic '65 that he loved nearly as much as he did his fantasy Ferrari.

"What's the problem?" he asked. "All we have to do is make sure we win two of the three volleyball games."

"Preppie, have we ever won a volleyball game in the past?" Slater asked.

"We've never all played together before," Zack pointed out.

"Did you ever stop to think why?" Jessie asked. She turned to Screech. "What happened the last time you played volleyball in gym class?"

"Well, actually," Screech confessed, "I haven't played the game in a number of years. Coach Sonski benched me when I was a freshman. I'm the official towel boy for the rest of the class," he added proudly.

"How come the coach did that?" Slater asked. His father was a major in the army, and his family had only been transferred to the Palisades area during his junior year. Now he was both a state champ in wrestling and captain of the Bayside football team.

Screech stuck his hands in the pockets of his wildly patterned shorts and rocked back on the heels of his purple sneakers. "I don't actually remember it all," he admitted. "I think my circulation was cut off for a while around the fifth time I got tangled in the net."

Kelly groaned. "Good-bye Smuggler's Cove," she said. "We might as well let the developers have it if we can't enjoy it after saving it."

"Never!" Jessie insisted. "We've got to save it no matter what. Who knows what Desmond and Deidra have in mind. They might change it. Destroy the ecological balance. At least with Inga, Ram, and the other surfers, it's safe."

Zack tried to take Kelly's hand, but she moved out of his reach, still mad at him for paying so much attention to Inga.

"Besides, all we have to do is beat the surfers and we can enjoy the cove anytime we want," Zack reminded them all.

Slater stared at his friend. "Were you paying attention to anything we said in the last few minutes, preppie? Screech can't play volleyball."

"Neither can I," Lisa added. "When it was offered as a substitute, I grabbed the ballet option rather than endure all those sweaty things that gym classes do."

"Well, four out of six isn't bad," Zack said.

"Actually," Kelly mumbled, "I haven't played in ages because I signed up for the ballet class instead of gym, too. It's so important for an actress to be graceful. Besides, I thought the discipline of ballet would help me more in the future."

"Three out of six," Zack said, his voice not nearly as confident as it had been. "At least I know Jess is a killer when it comes to volleyball."

"Er, was," Jessie corrected. "I haven't played in a while, either."

"You aren't taking ballet, too, are you?" Zack asked faintly.

"No."

He sighed gratefully.

"Tai chi," Jessie said. "It's great for getting rid of stress."

Zack collapsed back on the hood of his car. "Do they have any openings in the class?" he asked faintly. "I feel a stress overload coming on."

"We're doomed," Kelly said. "Do you think Inga and the others would take offense if I just sat at the top of the cliff to enjoy the view? Or would even that violate the agreement?"

Zack pulled himself upright again. "We aren't going to lose the right to visit the cove," he insisted sternly. "We'll just have to work on improving everyone's game."

"But—," Lisa began.

He cut her off. "Or teach everyone how to play," he added for her benefit.

"I can't," Lisa said. "I don't have the right kind of outfit. I don't even know what one wears to play volleyball."

"Anything you want," Slater said, "as long as it's comfortable and you don't mind getting it sweaty."

At Lisa's horrified expression, Zack hastily offered to arrange for uniforms. "And while I'm doing that, Slater can begin shaping you all up into super volleyball jocks," he added.

"Jocks! That's really sexist. I won't do it," Jessie insisted.

Zack motioned with one hand to the cliff path that led down to Smuggler's Cove.

"Well, I guess the word jock isn't all that sexist," she said. "It's all in the way you look at it, isn't it?"

"How much time have we got to become a championship team?" Slater asked.

"That depends," Zack admitted. "We've got to do some more research. Find out exactly when the city plans to finalize the sale, so we can come up with a schedule."

Slater sized up Screech, walking around him slowly. "Miracles like this one are going to take time," he said. "Time that we can't let Screech waste scoping out what the city is doing. We all need to be practicing volleyball until we're perfect."

"Exactly why we're going to move on to the

very next step," Zack said. "Jess, when is the next Green Teens meeting?"

"Tonight. Why?"

"Because," Zack said softly, "I think it's time that we all attended a meeting, don't you?"

Chapter 5

▲ ▼ ▲ ▼ ▲

The Green Teens meeting was held in the community center, but even though the room was large, it seemed overly crowded when filled with excitable teenagers.

Zack and his friends had barely stepped inside the door before Jessie was surrounded by eager members. Some even came up to Slater, remembering him from various protests or meetings that Jessie had dragged him to when they were going together. Zack and Kelly got separated from Screech and Lisa within just a few minutes.

"Here," Zack said, guiding Kelly into a vacant corner. "With luck, we won't get trampled now."

"I suppose," Kelly mumbled, her head turned away from him.

Zack glanced around as well, mentally counting how many more people would soon be involved in the Save the Cove project. He'd never worked a scam with this many people on his side before. Usually it had been him against everybody else. But here there were at least fifty or more kids, all strangers, who would be working with him. Now, that was power!

"You don't have to stay with me," Kelly said. "I'm sure you'd much rather be charming some other girl."

"Naw, I'm fine," Zack said, not really paying attention. Now that he thought about it, there were ways to use his talents in the future that were quite legal. A con artist didn't always trick people out of their money for his own benefit. Well, not just his total benefit alone. His ability to scam could come in handy for charities that held regular fund-raising events. Or perhaps he could lend his talents to a politician's campaign, making sure that voters loved his candidate when they got to the polls. Heck, he might even become a politician himself.

"Jessie can rouse the Green Teens to help organize the festival," Kelly said, "so you don't really have to stick around, Zack. You could go down to Smuggler's Cove and hang around."

"Hey! Good idea. The moon is full, the breeze is balmy, and the tide isn't running high tonight," he agreed.

Kelly sighed deeply. "So, what's keeping you? I'm sure Inga is still there."

"Yeah. The surfers are probably hanging out on the beach," Zack said. "Maybe we should go to Midnight Cove instead. It might not be as picturesque, but it's the same moon and the same ocean."

Kelly blinked. "*We?*" she repeated.

"Well, yeah. Who else would I be talking about?" he asked in bewilderment.

"Inga."

"*Inga!* Why would you think I'd want to spend a romantic evening with her?"

Fists on her hips, Kelly glared at him. "Why wouldn't I think it? You were practically crawling all over her this afternoon. You and your surfer talk."

"Inga's not my type," Zack insisted.

"She's gorgeous," Kelly reminded him. "All gorgeous girls are your type."

"Well, they used to be," he agreed. "But now I've got you."

"Oh, thanks!" Kelly stormed. "For all I care, Zack Morris, you can go—"

"What did I say?" Zack demanded, feeling a bit helpless. "What did I do?"

Kelly folded her arms across her chest, flipped her long, dark brown hair over her shoulder, and turned her back on him. "You know very well what you did," she insisted. "You insulted me."

"Me? How?"

"You said you didn't think I was gorgeous," Kelly replied.

"I did?"

Because he sounded honestly stumped, Kelly looked back over her shoulder at him. "Well, not in so many words, but you implied it."

"But, I—"

"I know how you are, Zack. You can't tie yourself down to just one girl. I know from experience, and I've decided that I'm not going to cry my heart out over you ever again." As if it were too difficult to talk to him face to face, Kelly turned away to stare unseeing at a poster that was pinned on the wall. It was of a whale.

Zack touched the shiny curtain of her hair gently. "You cried over me? Oh, I'm sorry, Kelly."

"I got over you, Zack," she said, concentrating on the whale. The photographer had caught it leaping from the water, its gray-and-white body curved in a delicate arc above an ocean so blue it was a mirror image of the sky above. "I promised myself that I wasn't going to let you make me crazy ever again," Kelly admitted.

Zack was silent a moment. So long, in fact, that Kelly wondered if he'd left her. But when she glanced away from the whale poster, it was to find Zack standing barely a foot away.

"Have you managed to keep that promise?" he asked quietly.

Tears rose in Kelly's blue eyes. She blinked rapidly, trying to keep them from spilling over. "No," she admitted.

"Ah, Kelly," he murmured, and put his arms around her.

Kelly hid her face against his shirt and sniffled. "I told myself it didn't matter if you did get interested in other girls. But it does matter. When you started flirting with Inga today, I . . . I . . . I think I need a handkerchief."

Zack pulled one from his pocket and dabbed at her tears. With her lashes wet, her eyes looked like glimmering stars. "You are more than just gorgeous," he said. "You are sweet, loving, kind . . ."

"Yeah, sure," Kelly grumbled. "Who cares about those things?"

"I do," Zack insisted. "It isn't just because you've got the best legs in all of Bayside that I hang around you."

"It isn't?"

"And it isn't the fact that every guy in school would do anything to get you to smile at him."

"No?"

"I love you, Kelly," he said tenderly.

More tears spilled down Kelly's cheeks. "I love you, too, Zack," she whispered.

"Then will you go steady with me?" he asked.

Kelly took a deep breath and bit her bottom lip. "I—"

The speaker overhead boomed to life. "Attention everyone!" Shelly Danforth, the current president of the Palisades Green Teens chapter called. "If it's all right with you, we're going to skip the usual meeting and get right to the heart of a new emergency."

As the crowd scrambled to take seats, Kelly slipped away from Zack and took a chair off to the side. Thank goodness the announcement had stopped her when it did. She had been ready to tell Zack that she would go steady. And she wasn't sure that was the smartest thing for her to do. How many times had she thought things with him were perfect and then found that they were actually far from it? It was just that she hadn't met any other boy she liked as much as she liked Zack. But that didn't mean one didn't exist. It was smarter not to go steady at all than to go steady with the wrong guy.

Except that Zack never seemed like the wrong guy. He felt more like the right guy. Oh, would she ever be able to make up her mind? she wondered as Jessie stepped up to the microphone. One thing was for sure: She had to find an excuse not to go to Midnight Cove with Zack. If she spent a romantic evening walking in the moonlight with him, she'd weaken and agree to be his girl.

Kelly fixed her eyes on Jessie. Maybe after the meeting, she could get Jessie and Lisa aside and talk everything over with them.

On the narrow stage at the front of the room, Jessie cleared her voice and looked out over her audience. "I bring ill tidings, fellow Green Teens," she announced, and hastily filled them in on the danger Smuggler's Cove faced. "There is no time to waste. If we want to preserve our natural heritage, if we want to be able to enjoy the glories of *all* our public beaches, I need you to help my friends and me now."

"What can we do?" a voice shouted from the back of the room. "Do you have a plan?"

"There's lots of things you can do," Jessie said. "And, yes, there is a plan in the making. I'd like to introduce you to my friend Zack Morris and let him tell you what we have in mind."

"Oooh! He's cute!" a girl behind Kelly whispered to her friend as Zack joined Jessie at the microphone. "I don't care what we have to do—if I'm working with him, I'll volunteer for anything!"

Kelly's heart sank. Did she really need to talk to anybody about Zack? No. She had to be firm and tell him she didn't want to go steady. It was senior year, and anything could happen next year when they all went off to college. She knew Zack's parents were hoping he would be accepted at one of the big Eastern universities. Since her family's finances meant she had to put herself through school, there was little chance that she and Zack would be together after graduation in June. With the whole width of the country between them, no way would he remember her. He'd forget she existed the moment he met his first gorgeous college girl.

Her mind made up, Kelly blinked back a new set of tears and listened as Zack explained his festival idea to Jessie's environmental friends.

▲　▼　▲

"Hey! Jessie!" Shelly Danforth called, pushing her way through the crowd of Green Teens members near the stage to the table where Jessie sat gathering lists of volunteer festival workers. "I want you to meet a new recruit."

The last time Shelly had introduced her to a new member of Green Teens, Jessie remembered, it had been a handsome giant named Sequoia Forrest, who had nearly got her arrested. This time Shelly was dragging forward a pretty girl with large dark eyes and long blond hair. Realizing that she had tensed, Jessie relaxed.

"This is Veronica D'Angelo," Shelly said. "She's a senior at Santa Teresa School for Young Ladies."

Jessie shook hands with the new girl. "That's a pretty exclusive school."

Veronica grinned. "Oh, it's just a school like any other, except that we don't have any boys," she said. "That's why I decided to join Green Teens. Not only can I get involved in protecting the environment, I can meet other people who want to do the same thing."

"And," Shelly said with a laugh, "it doesn't hurt that some of them are boys."

Veronica giggled. "It sure doesn't," she agreed. "Oh, but please, call me Ronnie."

"Welcome to Green Teens, Ronnie," Jessie said. "I'm so glad you're eager to help us save Smuggler's Cove."

"I can't wait to get started," Ronnie insisted. "But there is one thing I'd like to suggest be changed."

"What?" Jessie asked.

"The name of the festival. I think Save the Beach might be a better title than Save the Cove. Not everyone knows what a cove is, but everyone knows what a beach looks like."

"True," Jessie said.

"And although there are a number of coves in the area, what happens if one of the beaches that isn't part of a cove is endangered later on?" Ronnie asked. "If the city has considered selling off one of the public areas, it might very well think about doing it again in the future with something else."

"I hadn't thought of that," Jessie admitted.

"If the name was changed to Save the Beach, it wouldn't have to be just a temporary project but an ongoing one," Ronnie offered. "After all, it will take more than just a single festival, no matter how many Palisades residents come to it, to raise funds to supplement the park budget."

"Wow! You're right! I've been so worked up over this, I missed that entirely!" Jessie said. "What great ideas you have, Ronnie!"

The blond-haired girl grinned self-consciously. "I might be able to help out with some of the research that needs to be done," she said. "You see, my dad works at city hall, so I could head downtown after school every day and look for more information. He could tell me where to find what we need."

"This is wonderful!" Jessie cried. "Do you have any other ideas?"

"Well, I didn't want to seem pushy," Ronnie murmured shyly, "but I thought it might be fun if all the festival workers were dressed in costumes."

"What kind of costumes?"

"You said the name of this particular beach is Smuggler's Cove? So, why not have a pirate theme?"

Jessie jumped to her feet. "I love it! Where's that microphone? Ah, here it is. Attention, Green Teens! The suggestion has been made that we all dress as pirates during the festival. What do you think?"

The resounding "yes" echoed like thunder in the room.

"Boy, am I ever glad you decided to join this Green Teens chapter!" Jessie said.

"Now, if only I knew more people," Ronnie said with a sigh.

Jessie slipped from behind the table. "Oh, I can fix that. Is there anyone in particular you want to meet?"

Ronnie smiled happily. "Yes," she said. "All the boys!"

Chapter 6

▲ ▼ ▲ ▼ ▲

The next day everyone had their eyes glued to the clock, and even Jessie, who loved being in school, thought the hands were crawling at far too slow a pace. When the final bell rang and the student stampede began, the gang hurriedly dumped books in lockers, grabbed beach clothes, and dashed to the parking lot. Kelly, Lisa, and Screech all scrambled into Zack's car while Jessie hopped into Slater's truck. It took only moments to reach Gull's Head Beach.

Unlike Smuggler's Cove, at Gull's Head there were no cliffs and no picturesque rock formations. In fact, no one had any idea how it had gotten its name, but it was only tourists who really even wondered about it.

The ocean lapped gently at a wide, flat stretch

of sand at Gull's Head, making it a mecca for nearly every teen in all of Palisades. Because the land inclined only a bit from the road to the waterline, it was easy to reach. The city had built a convenient parking lot, and there were a long pier and a marina nearby with boats of many sizes bobbing on the waves. Gentle hills rolled away from the beach and were dotted with tightly packed rows of tiny houses, most built with balconies that had great views of the ocean.

Even though it was a weekday, there were a few surfers balanced on boards, riding the waves offshore. None of the waves was as spectacular as those at Smuggler's Cove, but Gull's Head Beach appealed more to beginning surfers or those who just surfed when they felt like it.

There were girls in tiny bikinis and guys in wildly colored trunks everywhere. Rather than swimming or surfing, they were all more interested in soaking up rays and flirting with each other.

Slater and Zack set up the volleyball net that Slater had brought in the bed of his truck while Screech and the girls did some stretching exercises to get warmed up. When everyone was ready, Slater pulled a coach's whistle from the pocket of his shorts and blew it.

Lisa jumped at the sound and bumped into Kelly, who fell against Jessie, who inadvertently knocked Screech facedown on the sand.

"What was that for?" Jessie demanded, helping Screech up.

"To get your attention," Slater said. "As the coach of our volleyball team—"

"How did you get that job?" Jessie asked, her brow clouding up.

"I gave it to him," Zack said.

"Why?"

"Logic," Zack explained, and got to his feet. "As Slater is the only one of us who is likely to get an athletic scholarship, I figured you'd all agree that he is the logical choice as captain of our team."

"I also am the only one who apparently knows all the plays in volleyball," Slater added.

"Okay, so I didn't know what a dig pass was," Zack said, "and you did. Or said you did. What exactly is it, anyway?"

Slater grinned widely. "You'll soon find out, preppie. But today we'll just be doing basics, so those of you who know how to play but are rusty can get back in the swing of things, and those of you who are beginners will become familiar with the plays."

"I can't wait to get started," Screech assured him. "In fact, I went to the school library during study hall and quickly memorized every term."

"Great!" Slater said, pleased that he had an eager student.

"I've only got one question," Screech said.

"Only one?" Lisa asked faintly.

"Do we have a doctor standing by?" Screech wanted to know.

"A doctor?" Jessie repeated.

"Oh, you don't think that the surfers will get violent, do you?" Kelly demanded.

"Golly!" Screech breathed. "I hope not. I figured having those spikes pulled out of my hand was going to be painful enough."

Zack dropped his head in his hand and took a deep breath. "Spiking the ball is just a term for a maneuver, Screech. There aren't any physical spikes sticking out of the ball."

"Wow! Am I ever relieved. I didn't think I remembered seeing any in gym class," Screech admitted, "but beach volleyball might have been slightly different."

"You're right," Slater agreed. "It is. We'll be playing much more aggressively against Inga, Ram, and the other surfers."

Lisa wrinkled her nose. "I don't think I'm going to like this," she muttered under her breath.

"Every one of our movements has to be efficient and accurate. Timing is super important," Slater insisted.

"Eww, I think I'm coming down with something contagious. Maybe chicken pox," Lisa said.

"More a case of chicken-heartedness," Jessie corrected.

"Come on, Lisa. I know that once you start playing you'll have lots of fun," Kelly told her friend.

"I hope so," Lisa said, but she didn't sound very sure. "What do we have to learn first?"

"Zones of movement," Slater answered.

Screech pulled a small notepad and pen from his shirt pocket and hastily scribbled. "Zones. Check."

"There are four of them," Slater said. "The high, the medium, the low, and the airborne."

"Airborne," Screech mumbled, his nose close to his pad of paper, then raised his hand. "How do we get airborne? Trampoline or catapult?"

"You just jump, Screech," Slater said.

"Jump." He scribbled some more, then looked up. "Do we need—"

Slater cut him off quickly. "No, you won't need plane tickets, parachutes, traveler's checks, or passports," he said in exasperation.

Screech's eyebrows raised and wiggled. "Interesting," he said, "but I wanted to know about special shoes."

"In the sand, most people play barefoot," Kelly explained. "But it's really more important to have the right stance, isn't it, Slater?"

"Absolutely right. And your stance, or waiting position, is in the medium zone, the zone you'll use most." He demonstrated it, placing his feet in a stance slightly wider than his shoulders' width. "You need to keep your weight distributed on the balls of your feet for balance," he pointed out. "Your knees should be slightly bent and your hands out in front and ready to move into action. Get up, Screech. I want both you and Lisa to try it. Zack, why don't you and Kelly help Screech while Jessie and I show Lisa the correct position?"

It took Screech no time at all to scramble to his feet and assume a very awkward-looking waiting stance. "How's this?" he asked eagerly.

Zack walked around his gawky friend. "Move your right foot this way a bit more," he suggested.

"And you need to lean forward farther," Kelly said. "That's right, but a little more yet."

"Your hands should be held a bit lower, closer to your knees," Zack advised, "and the palms should be facing each other, not pointing at the beach."

Screech went through some contorted-looking moves, trying to follow their instructions. "Like this?"

"Straighten your back more," Kelly said.

"Lean forward more," Zack countered. "Your shoulders should be in front of your knees."

"And your knees in front of your toes," Kelly added.

Screech straightened, leaned, and pitched face-down, his nose once more in the sand.

"Ooops," Kelly murmured, and had to hide a quick smile behind her hand.

"Er, maybe not that far forward," Zack suggested belatedly.

While Screech tried again, Zack glanced over to see if Slater was having better luck teaching Lisa the basic stance.

Between them, Slater and Jessie had managed to get Lisa positioned correctly, adjusting the way she set her feet and held her hands. They'd arranged her in the perfect textbook stance when Lisa pulled herself upright. "No way!" she insisted. "I look like a crab scuttling along. I'd rather be graceful."

Slater sighed deeply. "Maybe we should move on to serving," he suggested.

"Ah!" Screech said, sounding quite interested.

Lisa brightened. "Oh, I know how to do that. I play tennis, and Keith has been giving me some pointers to improve my game. Who brought the volleyball rackets?"

This time Slater groaned. "That's badminton, Lisa."

"You don't want to play badminton," Screech advised seriously. "I've never played it myself, but I've heard how it is played, batting poor defenseless birdies—"

"The game uses plastic birdies, not real ones, Screech," Zack said softly.

"Ah," Screech declared, giving them his most sly look. "That's what they'd like you to believe."

Lisa rolled her eyes. "So what do we use if there are no rackets?" she asked.

"Your hands," Slater said. Then he picked up the volleyball he'd brought along and tossed it to her.

Lisa turned her head away, screwed up her face, closed her eyes, and batted it away with the palms of her hands as if totally revolted. "Are you kidding?" she demanded. "I'll break a nail!"

"No, you won't," Jessie said. "If you do everything Slater tells you, your manicure will survive intact. And if it doesn't, surely Smuggler's Cove is worth the sacrifice."

"Do you know how long Nebula at Pails of Nails and I worked to get this perfect a set?" Lisa demanded, wiggling her brightly painted, long sculpted fingernails at her friends. "If she discovered I put just a tiny chip in one, she would turn me away from her door!"

"How unfair!" Kelly cried. "Well, if Nebula is that stubborn, you're probably better off without her."

Lisa shook her head sadly. "You know how hard it is to find just the right manicurist," she said. "Why, I'll bet yours is as particular as Nebula is."

"What manicurist?" Kelly asked. "I do my own nails."

"You do?" Lisa went into shock. "They're so perfect, I was sure you had them done!"

"Oh, no, it's easy," Kelly insisted. "All you have to do is—"

Zack cleared his throat. "Ladies? Could we get back to the matter at hand?"

Lisa blinked at him in puzzlement a moment. "Oh, you mean to volleyball. Are you sure there are no rackets I could use? If you knew Nebula, you really wouldn't want to get her upset, Zack."

"Maybe you don't have to," Jessie said. She tapped one of her own, shorter, polish-free nails against her cheek in thought. "You know, it might be a good idea to get some of Palisades' businesses involved in the festival. They could run the refreshment stands, sell souvenirs, or just benefit from having their name associated with the project. Being involved in the welfare of the community could be a big plus when it comes to getting new customers."

"Yeah," Zack agreed. "If we offered to advertise Nebula's manicure salon, she might even overlook ten broken nails."

"*Ten!*" Lisa gasped.

"It was just a figure of speech, Lise," Zack hastened to assure her. "Now, how about attempting a serve?"

"I'll even go first," Kelly offered, "and if I break a nail, you won't have to try it at all."

Lisa looked at her dubiously. "Wouldn't it simply be easier to find someone else to take my place?"

"No way," Zack said firmly. "It will take a major disaster before the surfers will let us substitute a player. If you don't play, then you can kiss romantic evenings at Smuggler's Cove good-bye."

"Eww. That's super depressing! Oh, all right," Lisa said. "Show me what to do."

Chapter 7

▲ ▼ ▲ ▼ ▲

The second day of practice wasn't nearly as bad as the first. Screech managed to stay on his feet, rather than his nose, and since she hadn't damaged even a single nail the day before, Lisa's mind moved on to fret about her hair and the strength of her sunscreen.

While Zack and Kelly held the court on one side of the net, Slater and Jessie stayed with their beginning player friends, explaining the different moves as they performed them. Screech kept careful track of the names of every volley and serve in his notebook until a ball he was supposed to get bounced off his head and knocked him flat.

"Perhaps you'd do better to get a book of volleyball rules instead of taking notes, Screech,"

Jessie suggested, hastily tossing his paper and pencil out of sight behind her beach bag.

"Are you okay?" Kelly asked him as she and Slater helped him to his feet.

"Yep!" Screech answered brightly, then blinked at her. "Gosh, Kelly! I didn't know you had a twin sister."

"Maybe you'd better lie down for a bit," Slater suggested.

"Ah, break time!" Lisa said, sighing gratefully. Before Slater could stop her, she had dropped down on the blanket they'd spread on the sand a short distance away and was soon recoating her bare arms and legs with lotion.

Zack and Slater had to help Screech to the sidelines since his feet and dazed brain weren't in sync at the moment. Once he was settled, Slater motioned Zack back to the far side of the net and suggested Kelly and Jessie get in some practice. As coach he would watch them and make suggestions on how they could improve their game.

Zack caught the ball Slater tossed him, and immediately had it airborne with an overhand floater serve.

"I've got it," Jessie yelled, and spiked the ball back across the net.

"Good one, Jess," Slater called.

Zack punched the ball, sending it skyward in an arc that curved in Kelly's direction. She jumped up to meet it, dropping to a low position, her forearms together to bounce the ball into the air again. Jessie leaped forward and smacked the ball over the net, making Zack dive for it. He missed.

"All right!" the girls yelled, and hit their hands together in an enthusiastic high five.

"Not bad," a familiar voice drawled from the sidelines. "At least for amateurs."

Screech bounded to his feet and was quickly at Inga's side. "Would you like to see me in action, Sunday?"

Inga surprised everyone by simpering at him. "Ooh, would I ever," she said.

"Er, I don't think that's a good idea, Screech," Slater cautioned.

But Screech wasn't listening. He scooped up the volleyball and sprang into action, attempting a jump serve. Except when he jumped to bat the ball into action, he missed it entirely and ended up on his face in the sand again.

"Oh, squid lips," Inga purred, hurrying to his side. "Are you okay?"

"Perfect, my angel," he insisted.

Inga brushed sand from his chin. "Are you sure? I wouldn't want you to overexert yourself in this sun," she cooed, and actually fluttered her lashes at him.

"Well, will you look at that," Zack murmured under his breath to Kelly.

"No, look at that!" she insisted, and pointed to the blanket where Lisa sat. Ram was rubbing sunscreen on their friend's back, and Lisa was grinning over her shoulder at him.

"Disaster!" Jessie hissed, joining them.

"Yeah," Slater agreed. "I don't like the idea that they came to scope out our practice session."

"They could have been here yesterday as well for all we know. There were so many people on this beach, we wouldn't have noticed them," Kelly said.

"But they sure would have noticed us," Zack added.

"Well, if all that is true, then why are they being so obvious today?" Jessie asked.

"And why are they cozying up to our weakest members?" Slater said. "I could understand Inga trying to distract Zack or me, but Screech?"

"She didn't seem to give a hoot about him the other day," Kelly pointed out.

"Other than to insult him by comparing him to a squid," Jessie said.

"Which he thought was a pet name," Kelly said.

"He's sure sure it is now!" Slater mumbled.

"Well, I can understand why Screech is being taken in by Inga. Heck, gorgeous women don't usually give the poor guy the time of day, much less fawn all over him. But I'm really surprised at Lisa," Jessie insisted. "I mean, she was dying to go out with Keith Bockman, and now that she is, she's going after somebody else."

"It's hard not to notice somebody like Ram,"

Kelly said. "He's so big and muscular."

"Handsome in a rugged sort of way," Jessie agreed.

"And that tan! Maybe I should try to get his attention away from Lisa," Kelly offered.

Zack frowned thunderously. "Megabad idea, Kel. You're not tall enough for him. I think Jessie should flirt with him instead."

"It's a tough job, but I'll do it for the good of our team," Jessie said.

Slater grabbed her arm before she could sashay away. "No way, momma."

Jessie blinked at him. "Why not?"

"Because Ram isn't the mastermind behind this plan to undermine us," he explained. "Inga's the one with the brains."

"And everything else as well," Zack said. "All right, I'll go flirt with her while you explain to Screech that she's just using him."

Kelly's teeth gritted together, but she didn't say anything.

"That's very self-sacrificing of you," Slater said, "but I think I should be the one to flirt with Inga. She'll like me better," he added, and flexed his muscles to illustrate just why Inga would prefer him over Screech or Zack.

Jessie glared at him. "I don't think that's any better an idea than my going after Ram. So, I guess we need to come up with a way to convince

Screech and Lisa that Ram and Inga aren't really interested in them, just in making sure we lose the match at the festival."

When they all looked at him, Zack groaned. "Why is it always me who has to come up with a plan?" he complained.

"Because you're so good at it," Jessie said. "This one has to be especially tricky because we don't want the surfers to catch on."

"Oh, right," Zack growled sarcastically. "Like they won't know the minute Screech decides not to have anything to do with the gorgeous Inga."

"We have faith in you, preppie," Slater insisted. "If anyone can pull it off, you can."

Zack squared his shoulders. "Okay, the first thing we need to do is—"

"Find Lisa and Screech," Kelly interrupted him. She gestured to where their friends had been but were no longer.

"I have a bad feeling about this," Slater said.

Jessie moaned. "Oh, great! Now what do we do?"

Zack ran a hand back through his blond hair in exasperation. "What else? We find them. And fast."

▲ ▼ ▲

They searched the crowded beach for an hour and never caught sight of their friends, but when they had dismantled the volleyball net and carried it and everyone's beach towels back to the parking lot, there were Screech and Lisa, sitting side by side on the tail of Slater's pickup truck.

"Where have you guys been?" Lisa asked. "I need to get home before my parents go ballistic."

"Your parents never go ballistic," Jessie pointed out. "They are the calmest parents in the world."

"And they know you're with us," Kelly added. "It isn't like you're off somewhere with a stranger." She paused. "Except that you did go off somewhere with a stranger. Don't you know that's dangerous?" she demanded, conveniently forgetting that she'd been prepared to go off with Ram herself but just hadn't gotten the chance.

"We didn't go any farther than the pier, and all we were doing was talking," Lisa said.

"Some conversation that must have been," Zack said.

"Well, it was a bit difficult," Lisa admitted. "He's a man of few words."

"That's surfish," Slater said, hoisting the volleyball equipment into the truck bed. "Surfers tend to use one word instead of a full sentence if they can."

"They can get a point across with a single word?" Jessie demanded in amazement.

"Hey, you've heard them, Jess. When Ram grunts *crucial* or *bizarre*, don't you know exactly what he means?"

Jessie pondered the matter. "Hmm. Communication completely with adjectives," she muttered.

Slater hoisted himself into the back of the truck. "For more complex thoughts you just add *entirely, totally, heavily,* or other words like them," he explained.

"And surfers never say *very,*" Zack added. "They say *way* instead."

"How do they ever describe something special?" Jessie asked.

"Like what?"

"Oh, the beauty of the shoreline," she suggested.

Zack shook his head. "It wouldn't interest them. The only things that matter to a surfer are waves."

"And those are crunchy, tasty, chewy, mushy—"

Screech's stomach growled.

"That sounds more like my breakfast cereal than a wave," Kelly said.

"Weird," Jessie said. "So, what did you talk about? Volleyball?"

"Space stations," Lisa said. "Ram wants to be a rocket scientist."

Jessie's mouth nearly dropped open.

"And what did you and Inga discuss?" Zack asked, dropping a companionable arm around Screech's shoulders. "The commodities market?"

Screech's eyebrows rose. "How did you know?" he demanded in surprise.

"Er, maybe we'd just better head home," Kelly suggested. "I've got a mega-amount of homework to do."

"Me, too," Jessie said. "Plus committees to contact to see how plans are progressing on the festival."

Within minutes everyone had piled into the two vehicles and were headed back to town. Slater and Jessie were quiet for the first mile, each thinking private thoughts. It wasn't until they were stopped at a red light that Slater cleared his throat.

"Uh, Jess? Is there something bothering you?" he asked.

Instantly on the defensive, Jessie gripped her hands together in her lap. "No, of course not. Why should there be?"

Slater reached over and squeezed her linked hands. "It's me, Jess. I know you well enough to know when you've got something on your mind."

Jessie shrugged. "It's just that the festival is—"

"It isn't the festival," Slater said. "So, what is it?"

Jessie sighed deeply just as the light turned green again. "It's Mom," she confessed. "I didn't even notice that we hadn't heard from Chance in a while until I realized that Kenyon Sinclair was interested in her."

"Chance is a great guy," Slater said.

"Yeah, I think so, too," Jessie agreed.

"You didn't always," Slater reminded her.

"I know. It took me a long time to realize that my parents were never going to get back together again, that they were happy leading separate lives," Jessie said. "Since Dad remarried, he hasn't had as much time to spend with me. In a way, I guess I was afraid that if Mom fell in love again, I'd lose her, too."

Slater nodded but didn't make a comment.

"With Chance living in New Mexico, he was sort of the perfect boyfriend for Mom, you know?" Jessie continued. "He wasn't around much, so she and I still had lots of time together."

"But it would be different if she was dating this Kenyon guy?" Slater asked.

"Very different," Jessie agreed. "Not only does he live here in Palisades, he's a super lawyer. I've been following his career for a long time. I guess I'd made him my idol."

"So what are you worried about? Sounds to me like you liked this guy before you ever met him, and you sure can't say the same thing about Chance Gifford," Slater said.

"I know," Jessie mumbled, then turned to face Slater, squirming beneath the restraining bands of her seat belt. "It's the idea that Mom hasn't said anything to me. Wouldn't you think she'd want to talk about what went wrong with Chance or what she hopes might happen with Kenyon?"

Slater laughed softly. "Listen to yourself, Jess. You're expecting your mom to tell you things like Kelly and Lisa do. I'm not sure mothers can talk to their daughters about their love life."

"Why not?"

"How would I know?" Slater demanded. "I don't have a sister. I sure don't talk to my dad about any of my girlfriends, though."

"Oh, but I suppose you talk to everyone in the Bayside locker room about them," Jessie countered a bit belligerently.

"Never did about you, momma, or anyone else."

"You didn't?" Jessie asked, calming down.

"So, have you tried to talk to your mom about what's up between her and Chance?" Slater asked.

Jessie looked back out the front window. "No. I don't know how to begin," she confessed.

"How about, 'Hey, Mom, have you talked to Chance lately?'"

"Easy for you to say," Jessie grumbled. "Maybe I could just eavesdrop the next time she calls Camille, her best friend. Even if she isn't discussing things with me, I'll bet she talks about them to her."

Slater turned down Jessie's street. "Talk to your mom, Jess. That's the only thing that will make you feel better, and you know it."

Jessie sighed deeply. "I suppose so," she admitted.

"Going to do it tonight?" he asked.

She shook her head. "Mom's got a meeting to attend and won't be back until late."

"Tomorrow then?" Slater suggested. "Call me afterward so you can talk things out."

Jessie looked at him in surprise. "Really?"

"Sure. Why not?"

"Well," she said, suddenly feeling a bit shy, "since we're just friends and not going together anymore, I didn't think you'd want to get involved in my problems."

Slater shrugged his shoulders. "That's what friends do, Jess. You need me, I'm there for you."

Jessie found she had to blink back tears. "Same goes for me," she told him. "If you need me to help you with anything, you just call."

She expected him to grin at her, to flash his devastating dimples her way, but he didn't. Instead he peered ahead down the street.

"Things might be heating up before you can get around to talking to your mom," he said. "There's a strange car in your driveway. An expensive black one, rather like I'd expect a hotshot like this Kenyon Sinclair to drive."

"Oh my gosh!" Jessie gasped. "It can't be him!"

But it was.

Chapter 8

▲　▼　▲　▼　▲

As Jessie jumped from Slater's truck, Kenyon unfolded his tall, well-dressed form from behind the driver's seat of his own sleek car. It was a low-slung sports car with enough power to make the person behind the wheel feel like they were flying a fast jet. It was the most difficult thing Slater had ever done in his entire life, but when Jessie greeted the lawyer and they strolled together toward the front door of the house, Slater tagged along behind them rather than linger to admire the wind-conscious curves of the car.

"What are you doing here, Kenyon?" Jessie asked while she fished in her purse for her house key. "Was Mom expecting you?"

"Not me, but certainly these notes about a

case she and I are working on," the lawyer said, indicating the briefcase in his hand. "I didn't realize Kate wouldn't be home yet. I guess I should have called first."

"She won't be home until late," Jessie explained, "but if you like, I'll be sure she gets the papers the moment she steps in the door." She pushed the door open and turned to invite him inside only to find Slater at her side. "Oh, this is one of my friends, A. C. Slater. Slater, Kenyon Sinclair."

Kenyon gripped Slater's hand, giving it a firm politician's shake. "Nice to meet you, A. C. Hope I'm not fouling up any plans you kids had."

"Nope," Slater said. "We were just stopping by to drop off Jessie's things before we went on to my parents' house for dinner."

Jessie was barely able to keep the surprise from showing on her face. Slater hadn't said anything to her about having dinner with his family. In the past when she had been invited over, it had always been on a Sunday, not on the spur of the moment on a school night. Then she realized Slater had invented the whole thing so Kenyon wouldn't think she would be alone. How sweet!

"Then I won't keep you," Kenyon said. He set his briefcase down on the dining-room table and flipped the catches up. It took only a second for him to remove a thick folder and pass it to Jessie. "Tell Kate that if she has any questions to give me a call. She has my home number, and I'm usually up until quite late."

"I'll tell her," Jessie promised. "I hope you weren't waiting long."

Kenyon grinned. "Well, I was considering ordering a pizza on my car phone, but you arrived before I had a chance to blow my diet," he said. "Although, now that I think about it, a pizza still sounds awfully good."

"Does it ever," Slater agreed.

"Too bad you both have plans," Kenyon said. "I'd invite you to indulge with me at Garabaldi's Pizzeria."

"The Molto Bene Special?" Slater asked.

"Is there any other kind?" Kenyon answered.

"Excuse me," Slater said. "I think Jess and I can easily skip leftover tuna casserole with my folks. I'll just call home to tell them where we're going, and we can be on our way."

"I like your friend, Jessie," Kenyon said as Slater slipped into the kitchen to telephone his mother. "He's a man of action. I've never seen anyone make up their mind quite that fast before."

"Well, where pizza is concerned, Slater definitely knows what he wants," Jessie said. "Are you sure it's all right if we both come along?"

Kenyon chuckled. "Of course. I'd like to get to know you better, and you'd be more comfortable with A. C. along, wouldn't you?"

She would, Jessie admitted, especially now that it looked like what she had feared was happening was actually happening! Why would Kenyon want to get to know her if he wasn't interested in starting a romance with her mother?

"I guess I'd better leave Mom a note in case she gets back earlier than expected," Jessie told him. "Will you excuse me?"

A moment later she was in the kitchen with Slater. She barely waited for him to say good-bye to his mom before she snapped at him. "What did you do that for?"

Slater looked confused. "You mean jump at a chance not to have to eat leftovers for supper? You don't know how bad Mom's tuna casserole is the second time. Dad and I eat it just so we don't hurt her feelings. Besides, I thought it might be easier to sound Kenyon out about his feelings for your mom than it would be for you to talk to her."

"Well," Jessie admitted reluctantly, "it probably would be. But the fact that he wants to get to know me better sure makes it look like he's got the hots for her, doesn't it? Oh, what can I say to him that won't sound stupid?"

"Isn't this the same guy you were looking forward to talking to not long ago? The one you were hoping would give you some advice about law schools?" Slater asked.

"Yeah."

"So, talk about law school," Slater suggested.

"And what will you be doing while I do that?" Jessie asked.

"Supplying moral support," he said. "And scarfing down as much pizza as possible."

Jessie rolled her eyes. "I don't know how you can think about eating at a time like this," she said.

Slater grinned. "One bite at a time," he told her, and dropped a fond kiss on her wrinkled brow.

Jessie's eyes widened in surprise, but Slater didn't notice. "Come on, relax, momma," he recommended, and headed for the door.

He'd barely pushed it open when the doorbell pealed loudly. "I'll get that," Slater offered. "You leave your mom a note."

Jessie hurriedly scribbled on the magnetic message board her mother kept on the refrigerator door. She wrote even faster when she recognized Ronnie D'Angelo's voice out in the hall.

"Oh, Jessie! I'm so glad you're here," the girl gushed when Jessie dashed out of the kitchen. "We're on the brink of disaster!"

"Calm down," Jessie said. "Take deep breaths, then tell me what the problem is."

Ronnie sank down onto the sofa. Kenyon put down the portrait of Jessie and her mother that he had been studying and settled in an armchair. When Jessie glanced over at him, he motioned her to deal with her breathless visitor.

"Well," Ronnie began, "I was supposed to sort out committee schedules with Shelly tonight, but she's come down with the flu."

"I'll do them with you," Jessie offered. "It's no big deal. See, disaster averted."

"Oh, that's not the real disaster," Ronnie said. "The real disaster is that we could all get arrested for even having a Save the Beach festival."

"What!" Slater exploded.

Ronnie turned to him eagerly. "Well, you see, you can't just have any big party on public property without getting a permit from the city first. And since we'll be making money at the festival, that takes another permit. Then, if you have any kind of entertainment, like the volleyball game against the surfers, that takes still another permit."

Jessie dropped down to sit on the coffee table. "We'll drown in paperwork!"

"It's worse," Ronnie said. "Each permit form has a fee attached, and they all take six weeks to get approved."

"But we don't have six weeks!" Jessie cried. "The festival has to happen in less than two weeks or the sale to Desmond and Deidra will go through and we'll lose Smuggler's Cove. What are we going to do?"

"Give up romantic walks on that particular beach, I guess," Slater said.

"Never," Jessie insisted. "There has to be a way

to surmount this problem."

Kenyon cleared his throat. "I might be able to help you, Jessie," he said.

"Oh, Kenyon! Could you?" Jessie breathed.

"You say this involves Smuggler's Cove?" he asked.

Jessie nodded. "We discovered that the city is planning to sell it to private developers."

"That would be too bad," Kenyon agreed. "You're quite right, A. C. It is a great place for romantic walks in the moonlight." He pushed to his feet. "How about if you tell me what you have planned while we enjoy that pizza. Would you like to join us, young lady?" he asked Ronnie.

"Would I ever!" she gushed. "Just let me call my parents."

▲   ▼   ▲

Kenyon and Jessie each had large salads, and the lawyer ate only one slice of the large Molto Bene pizza, leaving the rest for Slater and Ronnie. Jessie's appetite had pretty much disappeared. She sipped on a soda while the rest of them continued eating.

"And that's what we want to do," she said, finishing explaining to Kenyon about the cove, the sale, the festival, and the surfers' challenge. "I don't see how we overlooked the permits. Since Green Teens frequently demonstrates, we've had to get them in the past, too. I guess in all the excitement we forgot."

The lawyer sipped on a cup of decaf coffee. "It's understandable, Jessie," he assured her. "But you can't afford to waste any time on the paperwork. If you'd like, I could pull some strings to get the permits rushed through by your deadline."

"Oh, thank you!"

"Don't thank me until we've accomplished the impossible," he recommended. "The permits aren't the only bit of paperwork you've got, though, isn't that right, Ronnie?"

He caught the girl with her mouth full of pizza. "Mmph," she said.

"Those committee schedules," Jessie agreed. "Those are just as important as the permits."

"I have a suggestion," Kenyon said. "If A. C. can work with Ronnie on the schedules, you and I could get those permits in process tonight, Jessie."

"We could? How? The courthouse is closed."

Kenyon smiled a bit diabolically. "Not to someone like me. Let me make a few calls, and I guarantee the doors will be open when we get there."

"But I don't have any money to pay the fees," Jessie insisted. "I'd have to get hold of the Green Teens treasurer and she'd have to withdraw from our account tomorrow and I'm not even sure if we have enough money to cover everything."

"How about if I take care of the fees?" Kenyon offered. "Think of it as my contribution to the Save the Beach fund."

"Oh, Kenyon!" Jessie said with a heartfelt sigh. "That is so wonderful of you!"

"Let me make those calls," he said, and left the table.

Jessie relaxed back in her seat. "That's a load off my mind."

Slater munched on the last piece of pizza and stared at her across the table. "Not off mine," he said. "I'm not so sure you should go running off in the middle of the night with a man you barely know, Jess."

"It will be okay," she assured him. "He's interested in Mom, not me."

"I'm not so sure," Slater mumbled, his mouth full. "He hasn't said or done anything that makes it seem as if he's in love with your mother."

"Sure he has," Jessie insisted. "He came by our house without calling. That's pretty romantic."

"He was dropping off papers about a court case."

"That was just his excuse," Jessie said. "He wanted to surprise her."

"Instead, he surprised you," Slater pointed out.

"Well, yes. Oh, but don't forget he thinks Smuggler's Cove is a romantic place, too. Would he even be thinking about romantic places if he wasn't in love with Mom?"

"Sure he would," Slater said. "A guy's a guy no matter how old he is, and I sure think about romantic places every time I see a great-looking girl."

"See," Jessie said. "We're back to Mom."

Slater leaned over the table. "You're a great-looking girl, Jess."

Jessie's mouth dropped open. "You don't mean—"

"Why wouldn't he want to chase you, momma?"

"But he's old enough to be my father!"

Ronnie finished off her soda. "But he's super handsome and successful," she said. "And he's going out of his way to please you. I think that's really romantic."

"You're kidding!" Jessie insisted.

"All I'm saying, Jess, is that it might be a better idea if you and Ronnie worked on those schedules, and I went with him to the courthouse tonight."

"Oh, I was looking forward to working with you, Slater," Ronnie pouted.

"And you can't officially sign any paperwork for a Green Teens sponsored event," Jessie said. "You aren't a member of the board like I am. You're not even a member. I'm the only one who can do this."

"Just be careful," Slater warned.

Jessie nodded, but her mind was spinning even faster now. Kenyon couldn't be romantically interested in her! Why, he had to be twenty years older than she was.

Just like, she remembered reluctantly, her

uncle was twenty years older than his new bride. It had been a real shock to go to the wedding and find her new aunt was only a couple of years older than she was. Still, her uncle was madly in love with his wife and she with him. To them there wasn't a wide gap in their ages.

It might not matter to them, but it sure mattered to her, Jessie decided.

"All set," Kenyon announced, returning to the table. "Ready to go, Jessie?"

Jessie swallowed tightly and gathered up her purse. "I guess so," she said. "Where are you guys going to be?" she asked Slater and Ronnie.

The girl shrugged her shoulders. "I don't know. My mother has the ladies of her church group over for a meeting tonight, so my house isn't a good idea. How about yours, Slater?"

"How about the Max?" Jessie suggested. "I can meet you there as soon as we're done and let you know how everything went."

"Great idea," Slater said, and pushed his chair back. "Thanks for the pizza, Mr. Sinclair."

"Oh, please," the lawyer insisted, "call me Kenyon. After all, we're all working on this together, aren't we?"

"Guess so," Slater said.

"All in the name of romance," Ronnie said, and sighed wistfully.

The creases at the corner of Kenyon's eyes

deepened. "Anything is worthwhile in the name of romance," he agreed.

Mentally, Jessie groaned with foreboding.

Chapter 9

▲ ▼ ▲ ▼ ▲

Wednesday after school, Zack looked all over for Kelly and couldn't find her. He couldn't help but wonder if she'd had to rush home to take care of one of her younger sisters or brother. Since her mother worked full-time, if Billy or Erin or Nicki was sick, Kelly pitched in. Usually Billy, who was just three, was in nursery school, and Erin, who was ten, went straight to an after-school program at the local youth center. At fifteen, Nicki was involved in track practice or Spanish club in the afternoon and rarely beat Kelly home.

And if it wasn't that she was needed at home, it could be that Kelly had been called in to work at Yogurt 4-U, the tiny shop in the mall's food court where she worked part-time.

With her being so responsible and dependable, it really put a crimp in their time together sometimes. Zack hated that Kelly had so many different things tugging at her, but figured it was all these things that made her the sweet girl that she was.

It was a shame she would be missing their volleyball practice. It was very important that they play well together as a team. Even if they went down in inglorious defeat.

Too bad there wasn't a scam in the world that could take as uncoordinated a team as they were and turn them into champions who could sweep the surfers into the sea the day of the festival.

That didn't mean they couldn't do their best, though.

Feeling a bit dejected, Zack pulled his car into the parking lot near Gull's Head Beach, and got the shock of his life. Not a hundred yards away was Kelly, her shiny dark brown hair held back on one side by an exotic-looking flower, a brightly printed scarf tied around her hips sarong style, and a wide flirtatious smile curving her lips. She didn't even realize he'd arrived. She was too busy giving long coquettish looks to three hulking surfer dudes.

Zack sank low in his seat, his spirits sinking even lower. He'd been sure that she was ready to accept his class ring and go steady with him again. If the Green Teens meeting hadn't interrupted them, he thought she would probably have said yes on Sunday night. But it *had* interrupted them, and since then Kelly had been avoiding the subject every time she was alone with him. Which wasn't very often.

Now his hopes were totally dashed. Not only wasn't she interested in being his girl, she wanted to date lots of different guys. Why else would she be talking to three giant surfers at the same time?

Losing heart for volleyball just then, Zack started his car back up and drove quickly to the Max. What he needed was something to drown his sorrows, he decided, and ordered three giant milk shakes, one for each of Kelly's surfer dudes.

He was just beginning to slurp the second one when Jessie dragged in the door and dropped down in the seat across from him.

"Three shakes?" she said. "That means really bad news. I think I'll have one, too. Double chocolate, please," she told the waitress.

"What's your problem?" Zack asked.

"Which one do you want first?" Jessie eyed his third frosty glass. "Do you mind if I start on this one? We can share mine when it comes."

"Help yourself," Zack offered, pushing a straw and the shake across to her.

Jessie sipped. "Well, first there was the fact that Shelly got sick and Slater had to fill in on the scheduling with Ronnie. I thought that was fine until I found her kissing him last night."

"Uh-oh," Zack murmured.

"I know he and I aren't going together, so that's not why I'm upset," Jessie insisted.

"Uh-huh," Zack said, not convinced.

"Okay, so it's partly why I'm upset. What really ticks me off is that Ronnie is using the Save the Beach project for her own gain. She wants to meet boys, and that's all she's really interested in." Jessie gulped down more chocolate drink. "However, Slater doesn't believe me. He thinks I'm acting jealous. Can you believe it?"

"Well . . . ," Zack said.

"Then there's this thing with the permits. At least Ronnie told me about those before it was too late. Unfortunately, I had to get help from Mom's friend Kenyon Sinclair . . ."

Zack whistled long and low in surprise. "When you pull in favors, you pull in big ones."

"And that's another problem," Jessie admitted. "I thought he was sweet on Mom, but now I'm afraid he likes me, and now I owe him not only for getting the permits taken care of last night but for paying for them. You wouldn't believe how much those things cost, Zack! Kenyon peeled off a couple of hundred dollars in fees!"

Jessie finished off her borrowed shake just as her own arrived. Since Zack had drained the last of his own, when Jessie told him to stick his straw in the new glass, he did so. Nearly forehead to fore-head, they slurped.

"So why are you in need of antidepressant chocolate shakes?" Jessie asked.

"Kelly," he said. "When I went to volleyball practice, I found her flirting with a trio of giants."

"Hmm. I wonder if anybody actually turned up for practice," Jessie mused.

"If Inga and Ram had anything to say about it, I'll bet Lisa and Screech were missing," Zack said. "Which leaves Slater and Kelly. If she ever stopped giving those dudes her special smiles."

"And if Ronnie didn't come up with a dumb reason to keep Slater busy with her," Jessie agreed. "I guess we'll have to give up Smuggler's Cove even if we manage to save it."

"Farewell moon-drenched waves," Zack said.

They sipped chocolate to the waves.

"Good-bye swaying palms and picturesque rocks," Jessie said.

They followed with another slurping toast.

"So long soft sands and gentle breezes."

This time they finished off the shake.

Jessie sighed. "There *are* other beaches where we can enjoy those same things at," she admitted.

"True," Zack agreed. "But there is something special about Smuggler's Cove."

"Mmm. Memories," Jessie murmured. "Lots of wonderful memories."

Zack stared into the empty glass. "You want another of these?" he asked.

Jessie shivered at the idea. "I think I'm going to be sick to my stomach as it is."

They stared at each other. "I'm going to miss the place," Zack said. "Prom night just won't be the same without a trip to Smuggler's Cove. Of course, I probably won't be going since Kelly is more interested in other guys."

Jessie sighed deeply. "Me neither," she said. "Since Slater and I broke up, I can't seem to find any boys I'm interested in dating."

"What about Sequoia Forrest?" Zack asked.

"We never really dated," Jessie said. "And besides, he's no A. C. Slater."

"So we're both stuck sitting at home prom night," Zack said. "It doesn't seem right somehow. Maybe we should go to the prom together."

Jessie shook her head. "That won't work. For one thing, we tried to act interested in each other once and it was a big failure. We're doomed to just be best friends."

"Doomed," Zack murmured in agreement.

"And for another, it would be even more depressing to see Slater dancing with another girl," Jessie confessed.

"Or Kelly snuggled against another guy," Zack said.

"Maybe there will be something good on cable

that night," Jessie suggested. "We could pig out on popcorn and watch sappy love stories on the tube."

"Martial arts movies," Zack countered. "It's that or nothing."

"Don't be so inflexible," Jessie insisted. "How about a good space adventure?"

Zack lined up the four empty glasses at the end of the table. When the waitress came over to gather them up, she smiled brightly. "Is there anything else I can get you?" she asked.

"Five-scoop sundae," he said. "Hot fudge, marshmallow, strawberry topping."

"Warm peach pie," Jessie added, "and make it à la mode."

Zack leaned back in his seat and stared at the ceiling.

Jessie gazed out the window. "We need to do something, Zack. We can't just keep eating ice cream to cure our depression. It never works."

Zack sighed. "I'm scammed out, Jess."

"You just think you are. And if you really are, it's just temporary," she told him.

"I'll never win Kelly back," he said. "She's gone for good this time, and I didn't even do anything to push her away."

"Megasundae and peach pie à la mode," the waitress announced, sliding the desserts in front of them. "Enjoy or explode."

Jessie straightened in her seat, stuck her fork

in the pie, and was soon savoring the taste of it in her mouth. "You know," she mused, revitalized by the treat. "We're going about this all the wrong way. We've let ourselves get distracted from the main issue, and that's saving Smuggler's Cove. Even the volleyball game doesn't matter much. The surfers will move on to a place with better waves sooner or later, and then we can use the cove ourselves."

"True," Zack mumbled around a mouthful of ice cream. "So do we even need to play volleyball?"

"No, but we should just to show we aren't quitters. Besides, the poster-making committee has already made a number of signs advertising the game," Jessie said.

Zack nodded sagely. "Which means," he declared, pointing his empty spoon at her, "that we need to get Lisa and Screech back in the fold. We have to arrange for them to hear that Inga and Ram are only being friendly with them because they're afraid we'll win if they learn to play well."

"Exactly," Jessie agreed. "Then we need to show Slater that Ronnie isn't serious about saving the beach. In fact, if one of the developers got friendly with her, I'll bet she'd turn traitor and help them."

"Hmm," Zack said, forgetting about his melting sundae. "I'm getting the germ of an idea."

"Well, cultivate it," Jessie urged.

"It might not work," he warned. "Ronnie may not know everyone, but she has met us all and would probably recognize anyone from Green Teens as well. What I need is someone who is trustworthy, dependable, charming, and a stranger to her."

"Do we know someone like that?" Jessie asked.

The outer door to the Max swung open, and a tall young man with brown hair streaked with gold that nearly matched his soft amber eyes strolled into the restaurant. "I thought I recognized you guys through the window," Thomas Jefferson Racine said.

Zack looked across the table at Jessie. She smiled back at him happily.

"Jeff, old buddy," Zack greeted him. "Pull up a chair and join us."

Chapter 10

▲ ▼ ▲ ▼ ▲

Zack and Jessie avoided their friends on Thursday but were frequently seen with their heads together.

"What's up with Zack?" Lisa asked Kelly at lunch. "I nearly ran into him this morning in the hall, but he ducked into Mr. Pfeiffer's room when he saw me."

"Mr. Pfeiffer?" Kelly repeated, puzzled. "Doesn't he teach advanced calculus?"

"See what I mean? That's not our Zack. He may be calculating, but he's never interested in anything remotely related to math."

"Weird," Kelly agreed. "But I sure can't tell you why he's acting strangely. He's been avoiding me lately."

"You're kidding!" Lisa insisted. "He's been so

intense about getting you to go steady with him again."

"Tell me about it," Kelly said. "He asked me again Sunday night at the Green Teens meeting."

"And?" Lisa demanded, leaning closer to hear her friend's confidence.

"And nothing. The meeting started, and I didn't get to tell him yes or no."

Lisa shook her head sadly. "Girl, I don't know what I'm going to do with you. I'll bet he's avoiding you because he thinks you're going to say no again."

"You think so?" Kelly asked dismally.

"If you were going to say yes, a little thing like a meeting wouldn't have stopped you," Lisa said. "Would it?"

Kelly slumped back against her chair. "Oh, I don't know, Lisa. Sometimes I think nothing could be more perfect than being Zack's girl. Then an hour later he does something that makes me think it's lucky I'm not going steady with him. You saw the way he was the other day with Inga. It makes me nuts when he flirts with other girls."

"He's not serious about Inga," Lisa said. "He's just chased after so many girls, when a new one comes along he goes into automatic and flirts like mad."

"You think so?" Kelly asked hopefully.

"I know so because I do it, too," Lisa admitted. "Take Ram for instance. He's a hunk but that's all he is. There isn't a brain under that mop of sun-bleached surfer hair. Well, not one in working order, anyway. We have nothing in common, no future. But when he smiles at me and looks super interested in me, I forget all of that and go directly into flirt mode."

"You looked pretty interested the other day," Kelly said. "I mean, you disappeared with him for a while."

"And I probably would again if he asked me," Lisa admitted, then sighed. "I really feel guilty about doing so, too. It's so unfair to Keith. I mean, I'm crazy about him, and now that we're dating, here I am ready to blow it all."

"So you think that's Zack's problem, too?" Kelly asked.

"There is no guy who could ever be more in love than Zack is with you, girlfriend," Lisa insisted.

Kelly shook her head slowly. "I wish I could believe that," she said. "Because I really love him, too."

"So what are you going to tell him the next time he asks you to go steady?" Lisa demanded. "I want to be the first to know."

"Yes," Kelly admitted, but she sighed the word forlornly. "Oh, but what if he never asks me again!" she cried.

"Trust me," Lisa said, and patted her friend's shoulder. "If I leak what you just told me to the right people, Zack will be handing over his class ring to you in nothing flat."

▲ ▼ ▲

Zack lay in wait for Keith Bockman, managing to corner him when Keith came into the locker room from the Bayside tennis courts.

"Hey, buddy! Where've you been keeping yourself lately?" Zack asked, taking a seat on the bench where Keith had collapsed while he mopped his sweating face.

"Tournament's coming up," Keith said, "so the coach is keeping us pretty busy."

"Seen Lisa lately?" Zack questioned innocently.

"Only in passing," Keith admitted. "It's kind of hard to impress a girl when you're so tired you fall asleep in the movie theater."

"Ouch," Zack said. "Yeah, they never understand that sports have to come first."

Keith tossed his towel into his open locker. "I wish Lisa could come first," he said, "but if I want a tennis scholarship to California University next year, I've got to play winning tennis."

Zack shook his head sadly. "Same old story," he murmured. "Boy gets girl, boy concentrates on sports, boy loses girl."

"I suppose so," Keith said, bending to unlace his tennis shoes. He had one shoe undone before Zack's words sunk in. Keith straightened. "What did you say?"

"Girls don't understand that sports are so important."

"No, after that."

"Boy loses girl?" Zack asked.

"Is Lisa interested in another guy?"

"Oh, I wouldn't call it so much interested as . . . as . . ." Zack pretended to search for a word. ". . . as, well, fascinated. You don't have to worry though, Keith. I'm sure it's only a passing fancy. She'll get over Ram soon enough. In fact, she might be already."

Keith's brow was furrowed with worry. "What do you mean?"

"Just that Lisa is smart. She's bound to find out that Ram is just trying to distract her so that he and his friends will be sure to win our volleyball game next weekend. But she'll probably be so sick of all that romantic stuff at Smuggler's Cove by then that she won't mind not being able to visit there anymore."

"Romantic stuff?" Keith repeated faintly.

"You know," Zack insisted. "I'll bet you've taken lots of girls there. They get all mushy with just the sound of the surf in their ears and the feel of the sand beneath their feet. The fact that there is rarely anybody else there is probably a good reason to avoid the place."

"It's isolated?" Keith said. "And Lisa is going there with this Ram?"

Zack gave him a man-to-man smile. "Stupid name, isn't it? But maybe it suits him. The dude is certainly butting into your relationship with Lisa, isn't he?"

"Yeah," Keith said slowly.

Zack donned a contrite expression, as if suddenly realizing that he'd spilled beans that shouldn't have been spilled. "Oh, hey. I'm sorry. You didn't know, did you, man?"

"No," Keith admitted. He sounded pretty forlorn.

Zack clasped him on the shoulder. "Buck up. While I'll admit that you probably won't find any other girl as great as Lisa, I know you'll find someone, Keith. She might even understand about the tennis thing."

"I thought Lisa understood how important tennis was to me," Keith murmured.

"Of course," Zack said, "there is always a chance that we could open Lisa's eyes to Ram's real intention."

"We?"

"It would take two of us, naturally," Zack explained. "One to keep tabs on Ram while the other lures Lisa out to Smuggler's Cove. Oh-so-romantic Smuggler's Cove."

Keith kicked off his second shoe and threw it into his locker. "When?" he asked.

Zack grinned widely. "Friday night? That way you can ask Lisa out and she won't get suspicious."

Keith nodded solemnly.

Mentally, Zack rubbed his hands together. Two down and one more to go.

▲　▼　▲

"Come on, Screech," Jessie insisted on Friday night as she dragged him toward the steep cliff path at Smuggler's Cove. "This is the only time we can do this. In daylight the surfers would see us."

"We don't have to sneak up on them, Jessie. Sunday would be happy to see us," he told her confidently. "I'm sure you'd like her a lot if you got to know her."

"I'm sure I would," Jessie said, "but with the big volleyball game coming up, I don't think this is a particularly good time to strike up an acquaintance."

Screech gave her one of his more rubbery confused looks. "Exactly what are we doing, then?"

"Spying," Jessie admitted. "I asked you along because you're experienced at doing it and I'm not."

He brightened immediately. "So true."

Jessie didn't bother to remind Screech that Brandi Jarrett, the head cheerleader at Bayside's most hated rival, Valley High School, had noticed him lurking around her house and had been prepared with an escape plan when Screech and Zack kidnapped her before the big game. She needed to get him down to the beach and in position to overhear the surfers when Zack joined them around their bonfire.

"This way, and be careful not to trip over anything," Jessie cautioned. "I wouldn't want you to end up with any broken bones when you're so important to our volleyball team."

"Check," Screech said, and immediately stumbled over a vine.

Jessie caught him. "Shh. They'll hear us."

Screech pantomimed zipping his mouth closed, buttoning it, and then locking it for good measure. When he went to toss away the imaginary key, Jessie pretended to catch it and shove it in her jeans pocket. "We might need it," she whispered to him.

Screech winked wisely. Jessie dropped to her knees, motioned him down as well, then crawled along the beach closer to the circle of light created by the driftwood fire the surfers had built.

A few minutes later, Keith Bockman and Lisa crept up next to them. When Lisa started to say something, Keith hastily covered her mouth with his hand and cautioned silence.

Zack made no attempt to disguise his own descent to the beach. He even whistled as he climbed down. It was an old surfer song, Jessie realized, something she doubted Inga and her friends would mind hearing. Except when he went off-key. Of course, that might make them think their late-night visitor was another surfer. Or it might not.

"Aloha," Ram called out.

"Yo," Zack answered. "Crankin' fire, bro."

"It's the pseud," Inga told those gathered around the blaze. "What do you want?"

"Just paying a way friendly visit," Zack said. He settled down cross-legged between Inga and Ram on the sand. "Waves crispy today?"

"Insanely," Ram said. "Kona here totally blew out the inside section zipping for reentry."

In their hiding place, Keith got a stunned look on his face. "What?" he mouthed at Jessie.

She shrugged, no wiser than he as to what Ram had said.

"Way good, dude," Zack murmured, impressed.

"Don't patronize us, pseud," Inga insisted. "Just tell us what you want and then get on the road."

Zack leaned back on his elbows, apparently in no hurry to take her advice. "Okay," he said. "I want to know what you're so worried about."

"Us worried?" Inga echoed. "Show him how worried we are, King," she told a blond giant on the other side of the fire.

King laughed on cue. It wasn't a very cheerful sound.

"Well, you must be," Zack said. "Why else would you and Ram be hanging around when my team gets in a little practice?"

"Scope you out, dude," Ram said. "Way lame team. We're gonna shred ya."

Zack shook his head. "Not with our secret weapons gearing up to play," he insisted.

Ram frowned. "What secret weapons?"

"Ignore him, Ram. He's trying to psych you out," Inga insisted.

Ram's frown grew even fiercer. "Are ya, dude?"

Zack chuckled. "What do you think?"

"He wants to get you riled, Ram," Inga said.

"Dude's doin' a way good job of it," King commented. "You really got a secret weapon?"

"Two of 'em," Zack confessed. "Didn't Inga and Ram tell you about them? I figured they would, considering they've been heavily into psychin' 'em."

"Critical," King mumbled. "So what about it, dude?" he asked Ram.

"What about what?" Ram countered.

"Unreal," Inga murmured. "You're good, pseud," she told Zack. "I suppose the only way to get rid of you is to admit we were checking out how good you valleys are."

"And how good are we?" Zack asked.

Inga bared her teeth in a very unfriendly grimace. "Let's just say, I hope you're enjoying the cove tonight, because it's nearly the last time you'll see it."

"I wouldn't be so sure," Zack said. "You haven't seen Screech when he is concentrating on his game."

Next to Jessie, Screech swelled with pride.

Inga laughed harshly. "Squid lips? Yeah, he's

real treacherous. He could trip over his shoestrings even when he isn't wearing shoes."

"You seemed to like him well enough the last couple of days," Zack reminded her.

"Yeah, right. I've got him eating out of my hand, so even if a miracle happens and he manages to spike a ball just once, all I have to do is wink at him and he'll flub up. I've never had an easier dupe to trick."

Screech tried to pop to his feet and argue the matter, but Jessie yanked him back down and patted her pocket to remind him his lips were locked tight. Screech wilted.

"Maybe so," Zack drawled, "but that still leaves Lisa. She really dominates the net."

"That beach barbie?" Inga scoffed.

"Not hardly, dude," Ram said. "She's like way worried about what she'll wear, you know? She didn't even know what a dink was. She's cute and all, but no rocket scientist."

Zack snapped his fingers. "Oh, that's right. She told me that's what you're planning to be."

The other surfers all laughed. "Good one, Ram," one of them called.

"Yeah," Ram agreed. "Like my board is rocket propelled."

When Lisa lurched forward, her long nails curled into claws ready to scratch the surfer's eyes out, Keith tackled her and, in what Jessie thought was a brilliant move, kissed Lisa into silence. Lisa made no further attempts to come out of hiding.

Back by the bonfire, Zack pushed to his feet. "Well, it's been real," he said. "But I've got to get back. See you around the volleyball net."

Jessie waited another five minutes before signaling her group to move out.

Zack was waiting for them at the top of the cliff. He greeted her with a high five. Jessie countered by throwing her arms around his neck and hugging him. "You were brilliant!" she insisted.

"It's not over yet, Jess," Zack reminded her softly. "We've got two down but one to go."

"And he's a tough one," Jessie said, but she figured Slater didn't have a chance. Not with Zack plotting circles around him. Vaguely she wondered if Zack's magic would work on Kenyon and her mother. They were practically the only mystery she had left, and she wanted that particular case not only cracked but splintered!

Chapter 11

▲ ▼ ▲ ▼ ▲

It was Saturday afternoon and the weather was perfect for hanging out at the beach. So Slater couldn't quite figure out why Zack and Jessie were so determined to avoid being out-of-doors, choosing instead to be boxed up inside a restaurant in the center of town. Yet here they were, as determined as an honor guard, insistent that he come with them.

He glared at his friends and tried to slip free of their restraining hands, but they kept a tight grip on his arms and guided him through the dimly lit place and up three practically invisible steps. He tripped a bit on the top one, unable to see it.

"What's the matter with you two?" he snapped. "And what's wrong with going to the Max to work out our volleyball strategy?"

"This place is nicer," Jessie insisted.

"It has atmosphere," Zack said.

"It has far too many plants," Slater growled, looking around. "I feel like I'm in a jungle."

"Great, isn't it?" Jessie said brightly. "But more importantly, no one would think to look for us here, so our meeting can be top secret."

Slater let them push him down in a booth. Palm fronds brushed the top of his head and draped over his shoulders. "It's kinda dark, isn't it?"

"Dark?" Jessie echoed. "Oh, I thought secluded and romantic, but never dark."

All the same, Slater squinted at his surroundings, waiting for his eyes to adjust. "Hey," he said a few moments later. "Isn't that Screech and Kelly over there?"

"Where?" Zack asked, looking around. "I don't see them."

"Over there," Slater insisted, gesturing toward the windows.

"You sure?" Jessie demanded.

"Sure I'm sure. Kelly's wearing a short red wig, a pair of retro fifties glasses, and what looks like a hearing aid, and Screech's got on a phony mustache and is fiddling with a video camera," Slater said.

Zack shook his head slowly. "Too much sun," he murmured. "Cooks the brain every time. Those are just a couple of tourists, not Kelly and Screech," he declared as he unfolded a couple of sheets of paper.

"Why don't you look over these plays Jessie and I worked on last night?"

Slater wasn't looking at the plays, though. He was staring at the couple sitting at a table near the door. "I see Lisa's back together with Keith," he said. "I take it they are hiding out from Ram and that's why Lisa is wearing that giant hat and pretending to smoke, and Keith grew a gray beard overnight."

Zack and Jessie exchanged a look. "It's worse than I thought," Zack said. "The next thing we know you'll be seeing other people you know who aren't really here."

"You mean like Jeff Racine?" Slater asked. "He just walked in the door and he's really dressed up. It isn't often you see guys in pin-striped suits on a Saturday."

"Well, that proves you've got a case of sunstroke, Slater," Jessie said, "because even though Jeff is rich, in all the time he was dating Lisa he never once wore a suit on a Saturday."

"It's a good thing we brought you here instead of meeting you at the beach," Zack said. "Who knows how long these delusions would last otherwise?"

Jessie pushed the play sheets closer to Slater. "What do you think? Since Zack and I live next door to each other and neither of us was doing anything last night, we decided to work on a couple of ideas."

"We tried to call you, but your mom said you were out on a date. Anybody we know?" Zack asked.

"Would you like a soda or a sandwich?" Jessie interrupted. "Do you want to see a menu?"

"I want to know what's going on," Slater said.

"Nothing, that's why this is the perfect time to—" Jessie broke off and peeked around one of the palm fronds. "Isn't that Ronnie D'Angelo?" she asked.

"You tell me," Slater suggested. "Not a single person I've recognized is who they are supposed to be."

"Wow! It sure is Ronnie," Zack murmured, spying through the junglelike foliage. "That's strange. She's talking to that guy you thought looked like Jeff."

"Oh, and they're taking the table next to us," Jessie whispered. "I guess Ronnie didn't see us."

"Who could since we're buried in leaves?" Slater asked.

"Isn't Ronnie acting a bit suspicious?" Zack hissed under his breath.

"She probably doesn't want anyone to see her meeting that guy who isn't Jeff. That's why she came here," Jessie mumbled, her voice low.

Slater tried to get to his feet and found his way blocked on either side by his friends. "I—"

"Shh!" Zack and Jessie both insisted. "Listen!"

In the next booth, the young man in the suit was speaking. "So good of you to meet me today, Ms. D'Angelo."

"You said you knew of something that might interest me, Mr. Kinzelbach?" Ronnie said.

"I certainly hope it will," Mr. Kinzelbach replied, and gave her a slight smile. "I represent D and D Properties, the developers interested in acquiring the area known, I believe, as Smuggler's Cove. We understand that you are involved in this local movement to block the sale."

Ronnie leaned closer to him and played coquettishly with a lock of her hair. "You mean the Save the Beach festival?"

"Exactly, Ms. D'Angelo. We also understand that you are interested in meeting new people. Therefore, we at D and D would like to offer you a free membership at our new resort and spa," he said.

"Free?" Ronnie gasped before getting control of herself. "What's the catch?"

Mr. Kinzelbach widened his smile a bit. "The catch is that if D and D doesn't get the Smuggler's Cove property, there won't be a resort and spa. It would be a very exclusive one, I might add, Veronica. You don't mind if I call you Veronica, do you?"

Ronnie scooted closer to him in the booth. "Absolutely not, Mr. Kinzelbach."

"Alistair," he said. "My given name is Alistair."

"Will you be a member of this new spa, Alistair?" Ronnie cooed.

"All of D and D's management staff are members, as are stockbrokers, doctors, lawyers—"

"Indian chiefs?" Ronnie asked.

Mr. Kinzelbach looked apologetic. "I'm afraid not, although we do have two Arabian oil sheiks and their unmarried sons."

From her hidden position in the next booth, Jessie could see Ronnie's eyes glow with greed. Across the room, Screech had the video camera to his eye and was filming, his lens trained on the booth Ronnie shared with the fake Mr. Kinzelbach. Jeff was doing an excellent job of conning the traitorous girl, Jessie thought.

Zack was straining across the table, listening to Jeff and Ronnie, and even Slater, Jessie was glad to note, was quiet.

"Just what do you want me to do, Alistair?" Ronnie asked.

"Not me, Veronica. D and D. I'm sure you will think of something on your own to undermine the success of this festival. There are so many little things that could go wrong with the arrangements," he said.

"You mean like mixing up the schedules or losing the permits?" Ronnie suggested.

"Both excellent ideas, Veronica. But we at D and D don't like to leave things to chance, so we're willing to offer you a little something for any expenses you might incur." Jeff reached into the inner pocket of his suit jacket and pulled out an envelope. It looked like it was stuffed with money.

"But first I need to know that you are on our side."

Ronnie stared at the bulging envelope. "Oh, I'm on D and D's side all right. For a free membership at an exclusive spa, I'd do anything."

"That's all I needed to hear," Jeff said. He laid the bribe down on the table and stood up.

Ronnie grabbed it and opened the envelope. "Hey! This isn't real money! There's a geek's face in place of a president in the middle."

"It's mine!" Screech announced, sweeping up to the table. "I printed it especially for this trap, and now it's sprung!"

Jessie and Zack scrambled out of their booth, followed closely by Slater.

"Have you got the tape?" Zack asked.

Kelly joined the group. "Complete with sound," she announced, tapping the miniature headphone set in her ear.

Jessie glared down at a stunned Ronnie. "I'll be expecting to hear you've resigned from Green Teens," she said. "We don't need people in the organization who are dedicated to being selfish."

Ronnie tried to laugh it off. "Did you think I was serious? Ha! I was just leading this guy on so I could report how underhanded D and D Properties is," she insisted, pointing at Jeff.

"Right," Jessie murmured, her voice dripping with sarcasm.

"It's true!" Ronnie spotted Slater standing

silently off to the side. "You believe me, don't you, A. C.?" she pleaded.

"I would," Slater said quietly, "if I didn't know that this isn't Alistair Kinzelbach." He held his hand out to Jeff who clasped it gladly. "You're quite an actor, Racine. Even I was convinced you were serious about buying Smuggler's Cove."

Jeff grinned at the praise. "You forget. Swindlers run in my family. Since Lisa discovered my ancestors stole most of Palisades from the rightful Mexican owners, I've wanted to give something back to the community to atone for it. Zack suggested that helping to save Smuggler's Cove would be a great way to appease my conscience, although I haven't quite figured out how scamming Veronica does that," he admitted.

Since the plan had been more to get Ronnie out of Slater's life than to save the cove for the public, Zack made a point of not trying to explain things to Jeff.

Jessie had an answer ready, though. "We had to get rid of the weak link in our chain of command," she told Jeff. "The fact that Ronnie was willing to accept your fake offer shows that she would have sold us out if Desmond or Deidre approached her themselves."

"Absolutely right," Zack agreed, and turned back to Ronnie. "If you promise to have nothing more to do with anything or anyone connected with the Save the Beach project, we won't use this tape. But if you do, we'll make sure any new friends you meet learn exactly how untrustworthy you are, Ronnie."

"Fine," she snarled, and scrambled out from behind the table. "My grandmother has been offering to send me to a far more exclusive school in Connecticut, and the suggestion sounds even better than it did before."

As Ronnie stormed out of the restaurant, Zack clasped Slater on the shoulder. "Sorry, buddy," he said. "Although we need you to turn us into a winning volleyball team and didn't want you to be distracted by a pretty girl, we really couldn't let you get duped by that sincere act of Ronnie's."

"I understand," Slater said. "And I understand why Screech and Kelly were wearing disguises. What I'm confused about is why Keith and Lisa are."

"Oh, them? They were supposed to cut Ronnie off if she tried to leave before we wanted her to," Zack explained.

Slater raised one eyebrow in disbelief. "You realize they didn't even notice her when she stormed by a moment ago?"

"Oops," Kelly murmured. "They are kind of caught up in the romance of this place."

Slater shook his head as if he were still confused. "I don't see how any of you can think this place is romantic. It's just plain dark. Heck, I still can't see where I'm walking." He started to move off.

"Well, don't trip when you go down the—"

Slater stumbled and pitched headfirst into one of the empty tables, his arms outstretched to break his fall.

"—steps," Zack said.

Jessie flew to Slater's side. "Are you all right?" she gasped.

Slater started to push himself upright and flinched. "I will be," he said, "but only after I see a doctor. I think I've broken my wrist."

"Oh, no!" Kelly cried, and sank weakly down to sit on the dangerous top step. "That means . . ."

"I can't play volleyball," Slater finished.

▲ ▼ ▲

Once Slater was at home, his arm in a cast, and they'd dropped Jessie off at her house, Zack turned his car toward the Max before taking Kelly home.

"Want to share a malt?" he asked.

"Things aren't going entirely as planned, are they?" Kelly said.

"Some things are," Zack admitted. "I mean, the smaller scams are running perfectly. We got Screech and Lisa free of their crushes on Inga and Ram, didn't we?"

Kelly nodded. "Jessie told me about that. She said you were brilliant."

Zack brushed off the compliment. "And not only did we get Slater to realize how false a girl Ronnie was, we managed to make sure she couldn't foul up anything else."

"Yeah, and wasn't Jeff wonderful? Considering the things his great-grandfather did—or was it his great-great-grandfather?—Smuggler's Cove might well be named after a member of the Racine family," Kelly said.

Zack groaned. "Don't remind me of Smuggler's Cove. We don't have a chance of beating the surfers even if we manage to keep the city from selling the place."

"But Keith volunteered to take Slater's place," Kelly reminded him, "and he's nearly as good at volleyball as he is at tennis. Which is really good."

"That still leaves us with Lisa and Screech and only a week until the festival. It will take a miracle for us not to go down in instant defeat." Zack sighed. "I really thought we could beat the surfers, too."

Kelly brushed back a long strand of her dark hair as it whipped about in the wind. "Maybe we still can," she said softly. "What if they were already tired when it came time to play against us?"

Zack turned a corner and flew closer to his haven at the Max. Even though he'd come up with the idea for the festival, it had quickly become a plan that he couldn't manage. Maybe he wasn't cut out to run large events, not for charity, not for business. So much for that career idea. He was only half listening to what Kelly said, too busy wallowing in what would soon prove to be his biggest blunder. They were almost to the Max when what she'd said penetrated his brain.

"What did you say?" Zack asked.

Kelly grinned over at him. "I said, what if Inga's team was too tired to play well?"

"Hmm. That would even things up a bit. Good idea, Kel! Now how could we wear them out ahead of time?"

"With a surfing exhibition?" Kelly suggested.

"Whoa! Great! But how do we talk them into doing it without them getting suspicious?" Zack mumbled, busy turning different scams over in his mind. None of them were good enough, and what they needed was a surefire idea.

"How about if we get a rather pretty girl to flirt with them and hint that she'd really like to see all their fanciest moves on the waves?" Kelly said.

Zack pondered a moment. "It might work," he agreed.

Kelly giggled. "It already did," she said.

They were a block from the Max, but Zack hastily pulled his Mustang into an empty parking space along the street.

Kelly smiled widely at him. "It was so easy, Zack. I guess being around you so much has made scamming rub off on me. I got the idea after having to run to make it to government class on time. I was so exhausted, class was half over before I managed to pay attention to what Mrs. Tedesco was saying. So, after class I borrowed Lisa's new bikini, grabbed the Hawaiian print fabric I needed for my home ec project, and rushed down to the beach. I was lucky because Inga and Ram were nowhere in sight, but I met three of their friends . . ."

"The giant dudes I saw you with at Gull's Head?"

"Yes!" Kelly cried then sobered. "You saw me with Kona, King, and Fritz?"

"Er, yeah."

Kelly tilted her head to one side. "Is that why you've been avoiding me?"

"I haven't been avoiding you, I just, uh, had so much to do with, uh, with getting, well, stuff done, you know?" Zack insisted lamely.

"Oh, Zack," Kelly murmured. "I do love you." She leaned across and kissed him gently.

Zack took a deep breath, relaxing for what seemed like the first time in a century. He ran the backs of his fingers over her softly blushing cheek. "Then will you go steady with me, Kelly Kapowski?" he asked.

Kelly's eyelashes fluttered before she raised them and looked deep into his hazel eyes. "Yes, Zack, I will," she said.

Chapter 12

▲ ▼ ▲ ▼ ▲

A week later it looked like all of Palisades had turned out to support the Save the Beach festival. People arrived in carloads, busloads, and boatloads. To protect the beach itself, the vendors had to set up their booths along the road above the cliff, but no one seemed to mind the inconvenience. Everywhere they looked, the gang saw families murmuring over the beauty of Smuggler's Cove, children playing in the lapping surf, dogs chasing Frisbees, and lovers strolling hand in hand along the sand, soaking up the atmosphere.

Although Kelly had only talked three of the surfers on the rival volleyball team into putting on a demonstration of their fanciest boarding techniques, Inga, Ram, and a few others couldn't resist the urge to show off as well.

By comparison Zack and the gang only looked busy. Whenever one of the surfers saw them they were always involved in a festival-related event. But as soon as the surfer was out of sight, the real festival volunteer took over. It made the day one long scam as far as Zack was concerned, but his friends seemed to be enjoying the deception as well. When it came time to play, their team was going to be well rested as well as well practiced.

They were very well practiced, too, he thought excitedly. Although Slater was unable to play, he was still very able to coach them. While Lisa and Screech were still definitely beginner class players, they had melded well with their more experienced teammates.

And Zack had lined up a sponsor for the team.

"I really feel stupid in this," Slater grumbled as he worked his cast through the armhole of their official T-shirt. It was shocking pink in color and advertised Nebula's Pails of Nails manicure salon in bold letters on the front.

"Hey, Nebula swore to Lisa that she'd fix any nails that got broken, chipped, or damaged and never utter a complaint if we wore these," Zack said.

"You want a happy player, don't you, Slater?" Keith asked.

"I like the shirts," Screech announced. "In fact, I think my new sports jacket has a touch of this same pigment in its plaid."

Keith, who wasn't as used to Screech's wild clothing choices as the gang was, paled at the idea.

Kelly, Lisa, and Jessie joined the guys at the net, hair tied back with ribbons that matched their own T-shirts, their nails painted an identical shade, compliments of Nebula.

"Everybody remember what they're supposed to do?" Slater asked.

"Yeah!" Lisa shouted, bouncing as if she were about to go into a Bayside cheer. "We're gonna smash 'em!"

"Shred 'em!" Kelly said.

"Dominate 'em!" Jessie insisted.

"Rip 'em, whip 'em," Keith added.

"Blow 'em away," Zack and Screech said in unison, then did a high five, except that Screech missed Zack's hand, and he would have fallen facedown in the sand if Zack hadn't held him up by the back of his Nebula's Pails of Nails shirt.

"Exactly," Slater agreed proudly. "Win this one for me."

Screech nodded, then got the thoughtful look on his face that the rest of the gang had begun to dread. "What about the second game?" he asked.

"Why don't you win that one, too, Screech?" Slater suggested.

Inga and her surfing buddies didn't have matching shirts. They had matching tans and matching muscles instead. When they smiled at the gang, it was more like seeing wolves baring their teeth in a snarl.

Zack snarled back, as did Kelly and the others. Slater gave his team a thumbs-up.

The gang spread out on the court: Zack, Lisa, and Jessie in the front with Keith, Screech, and Kelly in the back. When the referee, the head of Palisades Park Services, blew his whistle, Keith sent the ball rocketing over the net.

Although it was barely half an hour since the surfers had dazzled everyone with their expertise on the waves, their enthusiasm for the game seemed to have restored their energy. Ram returned the ball, smacking it toward center court, where Slater had placed Lisa and Screech.

"I've got it," Lisa cried, and ran smack into Kelly. Both girls ended up sitting in the sand. The ball rolled free.

"Concentrate, Lise," Slater called. "Take your time and work up to your potential."

"Right," Lisa said as she got to her feet and brushed sand off her shorts. "You okay, Kelly?"

"More than okay," Kelly insisted. "We'll get 'em next time."

Actually, they didn't. The surfers won the first game.

"We're lulling them," Zack assured his teammates as they huddled briefly before the beginning of the next game.

"And they should be getting tired," Kelly added. "We're fresh, we're good."

"We're winners," Screech said.

"You betcha we are," Jessie agreed.

When Ram served the ball, Lisa and Screech stayed out of the way, supporting rather than hindering their teammates. The final points were taken when Zack dived forward to save the ball and got it airborne enough for Keith to ram it over the net and onto the beach before the surfers could react.

"We've got them on the run," Keith said, gasping for breath between games.

"You're doing great," Slater insisted.

"Yeah, but this is the game that really counts," Jessie said, wheezing with exhaustion. "And these guys are killers."

"Aren't they supposed to be getting tired?" Zack asked, breathing heavily.

"I guess they're in better shape than we are," Lisa said weakly.

"Impossible," Screech mumbled. "We're lean, mean . . ."

"Volleyball-playing machines," Zack finished. "Let's show them whose beach this really is."

"Yeah!" Lisa growled determinedly. "It's ours!"

But was it? they all wondered as they dropped tiredly into their waiting stances.

The ball was all over the court now as the surfers hard-lined every serve, tipped, dumped, and slammed. The gang responded with every ounce of their strength and a good bit more of determination.

If they didn't win, Lisa thought, she and Keith would never get a chance to watch the sun dip into the ocean together from this particular shore.

If they didn't win, Jessie thought, she would never be able to sit at the tip of the crescent, listen to the gulls and the surf, and dream about the future. Or about getting back together with Slater.

If they didn't win, Zack decided, he and Kelly would just have to sneak back to Smuggler's Cove. There was no better place in the whole world that was as perfect to share with the girl he loved than this particular spot.

The game seesawed back and forth, the score tied, then broke, then tied again. The surfers were wilting, but so was the gang. And then it was nearly over.

Inga leaped after a particularly high ball, caught it with the tips of her fingers, and sent it slamming directly at Lisa's section of the court. As if everything were happening in slow motion, the gang watched the ball in horror. It was so close to the net, traveling at what seemed to be the speed of light, and nearly impossible to stop. And Lisa, their weakest player, was the only person who stood between victory and defeat.

Seeing a future without Smuggler's Cove stretching before her, Lisa screamed what sounded like an ancient war cry and jumped, her hands out to block its trajectory.

The ball collided with her palms and ricocheted back over the net, burying itself in the sand between King and Kona.

The watching crowd went wild. Lisa found herself swept up on her teammates' shoulders.

"We did it!" she breathed, barely believing they'd beat the surfers.

"You did it!" Jessie cried. "You're a heroine!"

"Golly!" Lisa murmured, still stunned. "You know what? This was fun!"

"Wow, was it!" Screech agreed. "When can we do this again?"

"Soon, I hope," Lisa said.

"You want to what?" Slater demanded in amusement, laughing and hugging everyone at the same time. "I think we've created a couple of monsters, preppie."

"Who would have thought," Zack murmured. He handed around bottles of water to his friends. "To us!" he cried.

"No," Jessie said. "To Smuggler's Cove and the best friends any girl could have."

Slater tapped his bottle against hers. "To Smuggler's Cove and best friends," he agreed softly. "I'm proud to be considered one of those, momma."

It was just about the best day anyone could have, Jessie thought happily. Now if only her other problems could be solved as happily.

▲   ▼   ▲

After a quick refreshing dip in the ocean and a change of clothes, Zack swaggered among the festival visitors dressed like a movie pirate hero. His white shirt had ruffles on it, the sash at his waist was a deep crimson, and the tall boots he wore covered his tan pants above his knees. At his side he carried a sword that looked authentic in its scabbard and like really cheap plastic if he pulled it out. But he wasn't interested in behaving like a pirate. With his arm draped over Kelly's shoulders, Zack was happy just to enjoy the beautiful day.

Kelly, he thought, looked extra beautiful in an off-the-shoulder blouse and long maroon-colored skirt. Around her neck was a black ribbon holding his class ring.

"Ahoy there," Kenyon Sinclair's voice said over the loudspeaker system. "Is everyone enjoying this small piece of paradise?"

"Totally," Zack murmured.

Kelly grinned up at him. "You aren't reverting to surfer talk, are you?" she teased.

"Sorta."

"Enjoying yourself?"

"Entirely."

"And how do you intend to do things in the future?" she asked.

"Just the way you taught me to," Zack

declared, and reverted to surfish. "Treacherously."

"Crucial," Kelly said.

Zack laughed and hugged her closer to his side.

The sound system whined again. "As you know, this event is being sponsored and supported by the local chapter of Green Teens. And as you've probably guessed, I'm a little old to be a member," Kenyon said.

The crowd laughed.

"And you're probably wondering why I'm hogging the spotlight. Other than the fact that I have a bit of a reputation for doing so."

There was more laughter. Kenyon joined in it, laughing at himself.

"Today I'd like to share that spotlight with a very special person."

Zack and Kelly moved over to where Jessie was standing with her mother. Before long, Screech, Slater, Lisa, and Keith joined them.

"I knew quite a lot about this very special young lady before I met her," Kenyon said.

"Way special," Slater agreed.

Jessie gave him a nervous grin.

"What's up?" Zack asked.

"I don't know," Jessie confessed.

"I do," Kate Spano said brightly. She patted her daughter's hand. "Trust me. You're going to like it."

"I knew she was a good student, a wonderful daughter, and dedicated to the causes she believes in," Kenyon told his audience. "I also knew she had designs on becoming a lawyer in the future, so I made it a point to get to know her. I didn't know she was going to bully me into surrendering a good chunk of my bank account to fund this festival, or that she would get me so deeply involved in Save the Beach that I would be the one able to make this announcement today."

Kenyon paused theatrically and pulled a folded piece of paper from his shirt pocket. "I have here," he said, "a letter from the mayor in which he not only says the city council has voted against selling Smuggler's Cove . . ."

He had to pause while the crowd shouted and cheered.

". . . but in which he announces that he is officially founding a Save the Beach committee, made up of volunteers, who will continue the work that these great Green Teens members started. However, that isn't all my news.

"The Palisades Bar Association, of which I am a lowly member . . ."

The crowd chuckled at his false modesty.

". . . recently decided to endow an annual scholarship to one of our local, outstanding high school seniors. And I am extremely proud to announce that this year we are awarding it to the young lady who worked so hard to make this festival a success—Jessica Amelia Spano!"

Jessie's mother hugged her fiercely, as did Kelly, Lisa, Screech, and Zack. Slater kissed her.

Before Jessie could react to that welcome surprise, she was being dragged up onstage to accept the applause of the crowd.

She was still super stunned ten minutes later as her friends gathered around her, her mother, and Kenyon.

"Happy?" Kenyon asked Jessie as he slipped his arm around her mother's waist.

"Awesomely so," Jessie admitted. "But I also feel terrible because I . . . well, I . . ."

"She thought you were falling in love with her," Lisa said.

Kenyon grinned. "Well, I am," he said.

"You are?" Jessie gulped.

"You're a very special person, Jessie. Who wouldn't fall in love with your determination and energy?"

"Yeah," Slater seconded.

Jessie blushed. "I had kind of hoped it was Mom, you know, except that I didn't know if she was still in love with Chance Gifford."

"I'm not," her mother said.

"But that doesn't mean that you're in love with Kenyon, right?" Jessie added.

"I am, though," Kate said.

Kenyon smiled down into Kate's pretty face. "I've even gone so far as to ask your mother to marry me," he told Jessie. "But she hasn't given me an answer."

"Kenyon," Kate murmured. "How could I and not feel my answer would have an effect on Jessie's chances for the scholarship?"

Jessie looked from Kenyon, her hero and, she hoped, her mentor, to the happy, glowing face of her mother. "So are you going to marry him?" she asked.

"Yep," her mother said. "How would you like to be my maid of honor?"

Jessie stared at her mom in shock, then fell into her arms, hugging her tightly. "Oh, I'd like nothing better, Mommy," she whispered, crying happily. And she really meant it.

Don't miss the next HOT novel about the
SAVED BY THE BELL gang

SCREECH IN LOVE

Screech and Slater's cousin Vicky are in love. The only problem is she wants him to go with her to the military academy after graduation. Screech wouldn't survive basic training!

Can the gang keep him from making a huge mistake? Find out in the next *Saved by the Bell* novel.